HAPPY XMAS

LOVE

IAN & ELIZABETH

Storm in a Tea Garden

Storm in a Tea Garden

Alan Bayne

The Pentland Press Limited
Edinburgh • Cambridge • Durham • USA

© Alan Bayne 2000

First published in 2000 by
The Pentland Press Ltd.
1 Hutton Close
South Church
Bishop Auckland
Durham

British Library Cataloguing in Publication Data.
A Catalogue record for this book is available
from the British Library.

ISBN 1 85821 814 4

Typeset by CBS, Martlesham Heath, Ipswich, Suffolk
Printed and bound by Antony Rowe Ltd., Chippenham

Acknowledgment

I am most grateful to my friend Herbert Whittall for the advice he has given me on certain aspects of tea planting, tea manufacture and general tea estate procedures, on which, as generally a 'Colombo Wallah', I needed some help.

I have known Herbert for some fifty years and he has been a tea planter nearly all his life. After 'creeping' and doing various stints as an S.D. he became Superintendent of Kotiyagalla Estate in the Bogawantalawa district of Ceylon. So good was he at his job that he finished his career in the island as No. 1 of George Steuart & Co. Ltd., his previous agents in Colombo.

Herbert now lives happily with his wife, Joan, at Blackboys in East Sussex.

Foreword
by Sir Michael Walker G.C.M.G.

I was lucky enough to be British High Commissioner in Ceylon in the early 1960s. My wife and I spent three very enjoyable and interesting years in that beautiful and most friendly country. At that time the island was still called Ceylon and the mercantile and tea trade was still predominantly in British hands while the peaceful fabric of Ceylon had not then been rent by the Tamil revolution which overshadows life there today. At the time when we first knew Alan Bayne he was a leading figure in the insurance business in Colombo but as he had lived for so many years in Ceylon he had a comprehensive and detailed knowledge of the country, not only up-country on the tea estates but also in Colombo itself, which was the business focus of the tea trade where its main export was handled. Alan Bayne was an acute and well-informed observer of every aspect of life in Ceylon as is evident from his book.

The action of the book takes place in the period before the war when, on coming down from Oxford, Andrew Harvey secured an appointment as a junior superintendent on an up-country tea estate where, when he got to Ceylon, he would come to be known as a 'creeper', as were all new recruits.

Of course, in those days there was no question of a quick overnight flight to Ceylon to start your career there. The description of the long voyage with the stop in Port Said and passage through the Suez Canal may well evoke memories for some older readers who may well also recall that the voyage gave time for romance as well as watching the flying fishes. Just after his arrival in Colombo Andrew was driven to the up-country estate where he was to take up his post as 'Creeper'. There he met his Superintendent, who, as in all the major estates, was responsible for the growing and manufacture of the tea grown on the estate.

A 'creeper' has plenty of work to do. As well as learning the art of growing high quality tea, he also has to ensure that the army of pluckers adhere to the rigid rules covering the amount to be plucked from each bush, watching that they do not try to boost their take, on which their payment depends, by plucking rather more than the regulation limit, which would reduce quality. The other main aspect of the tea production is managing the factory on each estate when green leaf is converted into black tea. This involves a different range of knowledge and experience for the 'creeper' to master. However, planters are fortunate that they live in the beautiful scenery of Ceylon with its rolling hills covered with a green carpet of perfectly pruned tea in the midst of which stand the bungalows of senior staff, set in immaculately cut lawns with colourful flower beds.

If the 'creeper' is lucky, he may see something of the many colourful ceremonies which abound in Ceylon. The most important of them is the annual Pera Hera ceremony which takes place in Kandy, and where up to one hundred elephants parade around the town, escorting the senior and largest elephant carrying the Lord Buddha's sacred tooth. All the elephants are gorgeously caparisoned and they are accompanied on their way with much dancing and music so it is a noisy occasion.

However, there are, of course, other aspects of life for the newcomer in Ceylon. Indeed, Andrew found himself confronted by numerous difficult and embarrassing incidents, and finally with a potentially most serious development, which was happily resolved in a most surprising denouement.

The book is easy reading and I am sure that old Ceylon hands will enjoy the vivid and nostalgic scenes which the author describes, while the newcomer to Ceylon will find that the book gives him an authentic picture of the life of a young British planter before the war.

Michael Walker

Chapter 1

They were just an ordinary English family living in Wiltshire in an attractive old grey stone house, in some ways typical of the village in which they lived. The house was comfortably large and had been in the Harvey family for three or four generations.

It was at a sad time of his life when William Harvey moved to Headley Manor. He had only been married for a few months when he was told that his father was riddled with cancer and had only weeks to live. In fact he died only ten days after William had heard this tragic news. William's mother was distraught and begged her son to bring his wife and come and stay at Headley until her grief had abated. The young couple moved in, but William was shocked by the extent of his mother's bewildered sadness. It was a grim time for both mother and son, because William, too, had loved his father dearly. But worse was to come. In a few months' time the widow was reduced to an invalid, and she died of a broken heart. She had lost the will to live.

William and his wife Anthea had sold their small house in London and moved permanently into Headley Manor where their children Pamela and Andrew were born.

Despite the loss of both father and mother, happiness prevailed and the Harvey parents watched with pride as their son and daughter grew up. Public school followed preparatory school and Andrew eventually went on to read English at Oxford.

It was the summer of 1936 and Andrew was sitting at the breakfast table with his parents and his sister. He was feeling despondent and his whole attitude clearly illustrated this fact. He had just come down from Oxford, for the last time, and for the past year he had been happily engaged in wondering what to do with his life. The future had seemed rosy until a week ago when his father had said he would like a word with him and his sister.

They had gathered in the small conservatory on the terrace and, when his mother arrived, they had settled themselves comfortably on the chintz and bamboo furniture, adorned with colourful cushions.

Anthea Harvey had taken her seat beside her husband on the settee and put her hand over his.

Andrew and his sister were puzzled, but not unduly alarmed at this stage, about the reason for this unusual family conference. Their father had cleared his throat.

'It's some bad news – seriously bad news – that I must give you both. I'm so sorry about this and I can only hope that you can take it with the same courage that your mother has shown.' He had gone on. 'I think you both know that our family accountants are Seymour and Hedges, in fact my father used the then senior partner as his accountant. Since then I have been entrusting all my affairs to Horace Seymour's son, Walter. For the past month or two I've noticed that my dividends have been becoming fewer and fewer, and whenever I've spoken to Walter Seymour on the phone, he has seemed vague and hesitant in his replies. So, I called on him a week ago. I made no appointment on purpose. An elderly secretary greeted me and I could see at once that something was very wrong. This lady explained to me that the two partners had vanished and that she had no idea where they could be. She had telephoned both their homes a number of times but the phones just rang and no one answered. She was getting more and more worried and so, in desperation, she rang the police and they have started an investigation. There is no sign of the two missing men, or their families, but all the evidence makes it perfectly clear that they have absconded with their clients' assets, mine included. Unfortunately, Walter Seymour holds my Power of Attorney which means he can do what he likes with my shares and other assets.'

'What on earth will you do?' Andrew had asked.

'All I can do is to resign myself to the unpalatable fact that I have lost nearly all my capital. I have only my pension and some director's fees, and so your mother and I may have to alter our very comfortable style of living quite dramatically. We shall have to see how we go but we both hope that we don't have to sell Headley Manor.'

Anthea had then moved over to her daughter and, having put an arm round her shoulders, perched on the arm of her chair. 'We're so sorry for Andrew and you, darling. We had planned to increase your monthly allowances until you had settled down and found jobs, but all that is now out of the question.' She kissed the top of Pamela's head.

'Do you think that we will have to move from here?' Pamela had asked.

'No, I think we'll be able to stay but, as your father says, we shall have to watch the pennies. Also, of course, your inheritances have more or less disappeared.'

So it was this disheartening news that had made Andrew so depressed at the breakfast table that sunny summer morning. He realised that if his parents were going to live on a very limited budget in future, his sister and he would have to find jobs at once to help with the family finances. He told his father this.

'Andrew, I'm very touched that you and your sister have taken all this so well,' said William. 'Yes, we must all try and think of ways to keep ourselves going. The only trouble is that this wretched depression still shows no signs of lifting and jobs are not going to be easy to find. I feel better now that I've told Pamela and you of our trouble. Your mother and I have been nearly out of our minds with worry.' He picked up the morning paper he had been reading and, after a few moments, put it down and looked at his son.

'Talk about coincidences! Listen to this, Andy – here's an item in the Positions Vacant column – it says:-

"Applications are invited to fill the position of Junior Superintendent on a tea estate in an up-country district of Ceylon. Applicants should be between 21 and 24 years of age, unmarried and with a good educational background. Previous experience in a tea garden is not necessary."

What do you think of that, Andy?'

Andrew took a little time to read the paragraph. He read it more than once. 'It's lucky they say that previous experience is unnecessary, because I haven't the foggiest idea what goes on in a tea garden. They plant tea, of course, but I've never really thought about what happens after that. I'm not even sure where Ceylon is. It's somewhere near India, I know, but it seems very exciting, almost tailor-made. How should I apply, Dad?'

'Darling, are you sure you want to live and work so far from England?' asked Anthea.

'I haven't really had time to think but, yes, I'm quite sure. I'll miss you all, of course, but if I'm lucky enough to get the job it'll mean I'm earning money at once, and that's what we all need, isn't it?'

'Good boy,' said his father. 'Now, if you're quite sure you want to consider being a tea planter, let's ring this telephone number.'

They all walked through to William's study and, after a few words with a receptionist, he was put through to a director. Apparently there had already been a couple of applications, the director explained, but he said that he would be very pleased to see Andrew later on in the week and would he please bring his C.V. with him.

Andrew was a few minutes early for his appointment and he waited a little nervously until a secretary asked him to follow her. The director soon put Andrew at ease and, surprisingly, seemed glad that he had played cricket and rugger for his Oxford College. 'Not a Blue?' asked the director smiling.

'No sir, I wasn't quite good enough – I only played for my college.'

'Well, let me explain why I am talking to you,' said the director. 'We are known in this firm as London Agents. This means that we work in London to see that all goes well on the tea garden, or tea estate as it is generally called in Ceylon. Now, London is a long way away from Ceylon so we have what is known as a Colombo Agent in Ceylon. These Colombo Agents are in direct touch with the tea planter on his estate or tea garden. They see that he is kept happy and that he knows that he can come to them if anything is troubling him. They see his coolies are paid, that his teas are properly made and sold in the Colombo market or shipped to London, they insure his tea factory and so on.'

After the interview Andrew was told that he would hear from the London Agents in a few days' time. In fact he heard the next morning and he was excited and delighted to read from the letter that he had got the job. His excitement now knew no bounds.

The letter set out details of the terms on which he would be employed and, to his mother's consternation, he discovered his first agreement would be for a period of five years – a long time to be away from England. The London Agents said that a first class passage would be booked for him on a P & O or other ship leaving for Colombo in a month's time and, in that interval, would he please secure a passport, have all the necessary injections and buy some tropical clothes with the allowance they would give him.

It seemed no time at all before Andrew was standing on the quay at Tilbury gazing up at the enormous white hull of the liner that was to take him to Ceylon. His mother had tried her best to look cheerful, for Andrew's sake, but she felt that her heart was breaking at the thought of losing her son for five years.

Andrew watched his luggage go on board and then said goodbye to his parents at the gangway. This was not easy, and he felt decidedly weepy as he turned away.

A steward greeted Andrew as he stepped on board and asked his name. After a quick look at the list he was holding he said, 'Welcome aboard, sir. Please follow me and I will show you to your cabin. Your luggage will be with you quite soon.'

Andrew's cabin was fairly small, but at least it had a porthole and was comfortably furnished. After a few moments there was a knock on the door and another steward entered. 'Good morning, sir.' he said and went on: 'My name is Dawson and I will be looking after you until we reach Colombo. Would you like me to unpack for you or would you rather do it yourself?'

Andrew said he would prefer to unpack himself and Dawson said, 'Very good sir. Your bathroom is just along the passage here. You will have another steward who will run a bath for you whenever you want one. You'll probably want more than one a day when we leave the Suez Canal and enter the Red Sea. Your bathroom steward is an Indian, a Goanese in fact from the West Coast of India. Another thing, sir. You'll find that your bath water is salt water. Fresh water is scarce at sea, but sea water is always around us. However, in your bathroom you'll find a small basin which you can fill with fresh water whenever you want. Please ring this bell for anything you need. We're due to sail at five this evening on the tide.' He then departed.

Andrew had only been left alone for a few minutes when there was another knock on the door – a rather grand looking officer entered. 'Good morning Mr Harvey,' he said. 'I'm the Purser and I've just looked in to see if you are comfortable and have everything you want.'

This was only partly the truth. What the Purser didn't tell Andrew was that, because the ship was about to start on her maiden voyage, the Company Chairman and his wife and daughter would be sailing with them. The Chairman had said casually, a week or two earlier, that his twenty-year-old daughter had hoped she would meet some nice young men on board, apart from the officers of course. On looking through the passenger list the Purser thought Andrew might be a suitable choice to sit at the Captain's table next to the Chairman's daughter and so, despite being frantically busy with embarkation in full swing, he decided to check him out. After chatting for five minutes the Purser left and, more than satisfied, decided to put Andrew at the Captain's table, sitting next to Sarah Allenby.

There was a note in Andrew's cabin telling him that seating at lunch had not been allocated and he could sit where he liked. He was also reminded that, whilst in port, or the first night at sea, a dinner jacket and a black tie were not obligatory at dinner, but otherwise they were. Finally he was told that he would be at the second sitting for all his meals. Although he didn't know it at the time, the second sitting was preferred by most of the seasoned passengers because the first sitting for dinner was too early, usually seven o'clock. As his luggage had not yet arrived, Andrew went for a walk of discovery round the ship and he was staggered at the size and luxuriousness of all he saw.

After lunch he went down to his cabin, unpacked and then sat on deck watching the other passengers exploring the ship. The crew were busy preparing the ship for its voyage. At half past four the announcement, 'All visitors ashore please' was made, and just after five o'clock Andrew felt the steady rhythm of the giant engines under his feet as the great ship moved slowly off and headed for the sea.

Whilst Andrew was changing for dinner his steward looked in to see if he had everything he wanted.

'There's just one thing,' said Andrew. 'I'm not too sure about this "first" and "second" sitting business. What's it all about?'

'Well, sir,' said Dawson, 'the ship's absolutely full and the dining saloon is not big enough to hold all the first class passengers on board at one sitting. So we have two sittings for all meals, the second sitting, your one, is an hour and a half after the first, but don't worry, you'll hear a bugle and then an announcement over the tannoy telling you when to go down. I can tell you, sir, that you've been put at the Captain's table so you shouldn't be late or he might get cross! Only joking, sir.'

Andrew wondered why on earth he had been put at the Captain's table. He knew the ship was on her maiden voyage but this did not explain why this honour had been conferred upon him. He was soon to find out.

Half an hour or so before dinner, Andrew went to one of the three main bars and ordered a glass of sherry. At eight thirty the second sitting dinner was announced, as the steward had said, and he made his way to the dining saloon. The Chief Steward greeted him, asked his name, and said immediately, 'Follow me, sir.'

Andrew did as he was bid and saw the Captain standing beside his table talking to a middle-aged man and his wife. A lovely young girl was there too.

The Chief Steward left without a word and the Captain came forward. He smiled and put out his hand. 'You must be Andrew Harvey

6

– I am Captain Masterton and this is Sir Colin Allenby, the Chairman of the Company, Lady Allenby and Miss Sarah Allenby.'

Andrew shook hands and turned to Sarah Allenby as the Captain and his two principal guests moved away to greet the six other passengers who were to sit with them.

Sarah Allenby was of medium height and had a head of wonderful auburn hair. Her eyes were greenish-grey and she had the hint of a freckle here and there. She was very pretty. She looked up at Andrew and very much liked what she saw. This was a young man about six feet three inches tall with blue eyes and brown hair that had the suggestion of a wave in it. He had an engaging smile which somehow thrilled her.

The other passengers at the table were early-middle-aged and were all bound for Singapore and Australia.

A steward handed the menu to Andrew. Never before had he seen such a vast selection of food. He turned to Sarah and whispered, 'Is this just for tonight, or is it for the whole voyage?'

She giggled. 'It's for this evening, and breakfast and lunch are just as enormous.'

The passenger on Andrew's right was charming and chatted away happily whenever she could claim Andrew's attention. This, however, was not the case with one of the other ladies at the table. She was artificial from her head to her toes and she couldn't take her eyes off Andrew. Andrew thought that she might have been about fifty years old, and she was much younger than her husband, who seemed rather frail and not in the best of health. They were Americans, and clearly had had a longish session in one of the bars before dinner. Andrew was more than surprised when, at one stage during the meal, the lady raised her glass in silence towards him, drank, and gave him a very knowing look, a clear indication that she wanted to see more of him. This was something quite new to Andrew; he was now twenty-three and had had the normal run of flirtations and minor affairs at Oxford, but this was an opening move he had not encountered before.

'Don't look now, but who is the lady in the green dress?' he whispered to Sarah.

'I don't really know, but I do know they're Americans and their name is Jepson. Why do you ask?'

'Because she's staring at me a lot in a funny way and I'm getting nervous!'

'Well, you concentrate on me. May I call you Andrew? Yes, you concentrate on me and you'll come to no harm.' She leant towards him. 'Or not much,' she whispered, 'and if you have any more trouble from your green lady opposite I'll get my father to put her ashore at Gibraltar! How dare she behave like that. I saw you first, anyway!'

Andrew was delighted that Sarah was teasing him – he loved it. 'Yes, please call me Andrew, or Andy. I answer to both, and you're Sarah, aren't you?'

'Yes, that's right. Would you like to join my parents and me for coffee after dinner?'

'I'd love to. I'll follow you out like a pet poodle!'

'You do that!' said Sarah, and started to pay more attention to the 'green lady' opposite. It was quite true – she was staring at Andrew a lot.

After coffee in the ship's main lounge Sarah suggested a walk on deck. Both she and Andrew went out, and the girl pointed to a companionway. 'This way, Andy – it leads to the boat deck.'

'You seem to know your way around pretty well, considering we've only been on board for a few hours!' remarked Andrew.

'I should,' said Sarah, putting a dainty foot on the first step of the companionway, 'I came on board several times whilst she was being built and fitted out.' She went on: 'And another thing. I seem to have been on ocean voyages for ever. Summer holidays, winter holidays, the lot. My father has always been a steamship man.'

It was a lovely summer's evening and the sea was dead calm – there was just the rustle and splash from the bow-wave of the ship – the Bay of Biscay and its notorious roughness still lay ahead. After strolling for a few minutes Andrew instinctively put his arm through Sarah's. She brought up her free hand and held his. She looked up. 'That's quick work, Andy – don't forget I'm the Chairman's daughter and I can have you put in irons and cast into some dark dungeon!' she joked.

'I don't care if you're the King of Siam's daughter. I've wanted to do this since dinner and I'm going to go on doing it.'

'Good boy – what do you think of this?' She turned towards him, drew down his head and kissed him full on the mouth. They finally untangled themselves and moved to the rail. 'Wow!' said Andrew.

After a while they joined Sarah's parents, and Andrew said he was going to turn in. Sarah looked radiant and this fact did not escape her mother who hid a little smile.

In his cabin, Andrew opened the porthole and gazed out to sea. It was dark now and the moon was rising over the French coast. His thoughts were very much concentrated on Sarah. The thing that struck

8

him most was the fact that, although she gave the impression that she was older than her twenty years, and that she was very self assured, there was simply no conceit in her make-up. He found Sarah genuinely natural and very affectionate. She was lovely to look at, but she didn't trade on this asset. Andrew decided there was a paradox here: Sarah appeared sophisticated but her nature was unsophistication itself.

There was a knock on the door. His heart leapt and he opened the door beaming with delight, but not for long. It was the 'green lady' from the Captain's table. She came straight into the cabin, gently pushing Andrew aside and closing the door behind her.

'Good evening,' she said.

Andrew was still a very young man and this was a situation which he had no idea how to handle. His immediate reactions of surprise and disappointment showed in his face.

'You don't seem very pleased to see me – let me introduce myself. My name is Cynthia Jepson' – She moved over to Andrew's bed and sat on it – 'and I'm disappointed that you did not respond to the little toast I gave you with my wine glass at dinner.'

'I don't know why you're in my cabin at this late hour – have you come here by mistake?'

'Oh, come on, Andrew, grow up. Why do you think a lady visits a gentleman's cabin late at night? You're not so innocent. I watched you with the Chairman's daughter at dinner and I'd like to know where you both disappeared to after dinner. Please, Andrew, be kind to me, I'm very lonely. Oh yes, I have a husband on board but he is old and not very well, and he's no good to me as a husband. Now *you*, you would be very, very good for me. Look, I'll show you.'

The 'green lady' was out of her green dress in a flash. She showed no signs of her fifty or so years. Her figure was good, and the black silk bra and panties she was wearing certainly had an alarmingly quick effect on Andrew.

He pulled himself together. 'Please put your dress on . . .' But that was as far as he got.

Cynthia Jepson flew at him and smothered him with kisses, dragging him to the bed and groping for his flies. But he brushed her hand aside and disengaged himself.

'Please dress and go, Mrs Jepson, and please never do this again!'

'Why not? What will you do if I decide to come to your cabin every night? Will you report me to the Captain, or will you tell your little girlfriend instead? Tell her by all means. I'll say that you asked me to come, *begged* me to come. I'll say that you tried to rape me!

Oh, come on, Andrew, take your clothes off and just give me a little hug. I need it very badly. Please make love to me.'

'I'm going on deck. Please be gone by the time I come back and please never come near me again,' Andrew snapped, slamming the door on his way out.

'You bastard!' said Mrs Jepson to herself.

Andrew went on deck and bumped into the Allenby family who were having a final stroll before turning in. 'I thought you were going to bed, Andy,' said Sarah.

'Well, I was looking out through my porthole and it seemed such a lovely night that I thought I'd have another half hour on deck.'

'What about meeting me by the pool tomorrow morning for a swim before breakfast?' asked Sarah. 'Say, eight o'clock?'

'Fine. I'll be there. I'll look forward to it.'

After a little while Andrew went down to his cabin hoping Cynthia Jepson had gone. She had, but on his dressing table was an envelope. He opened it and written on ship's paper was a brief note:

'Darling Andrew,
    Please don't be too cross with me. I must have had too much to drink at dinner. This comes with my love – please accept it.
C.'

A cheque for ten thousand dollars was enclosed. Andrew stared at it in disbelief. He put the note and the cheque back in the envelope and hid them under some clothes in his chest of drawers. He undressed and lay on his bed unable to sleep. 'What a mess,' he thought to himself. 'What on earth do I do?'

Finally, he fell asleep.

Sarah was waiting by the pool when Andrew arrived, and so was Cynthia Jepson, who was chatting to Sarah. As calmly as he could, Andrew said, 'Good morning.'

Sarah, unknowingly, saved him further embarrassment by saying, 'Come on, Andy – I'll race you over ten lengths,' and they dived in.

Andrew had done a good deal of thinking before he went to sleep the previous evening, and his thoughts were busy again this morning from the moment he woke up. He wondered what to do about Cynthia Jepson's little note and her cheque. The answer came to him whilst he was having a bath after his swim.

At about eleven o'clock that morning he saw Sir Colin and Lady

Allenby walking round the deck. He went up to them. 'Forgive me, sir,' he said to Sir Colin, 'but I wonder if I could have a word with you?'

'Yes Andrew, of course. Let's find some chairs and then you can fire away.'

Lady Allenby's first thought was that it was something to do with Sarah, but she soon dismissed the idea. *They can't possibly be in love or engaged already*, she decided.

The three settled themselves, and Andrew came straight to the point. 'It's about a passenger, sir, a Mrs Jepson, who sits at our table. During dinner last night she was staring at me almost continuously and even Sarah noticed. Well, after I went to my cabin, to go to bed, there was a knock on the door and it was Mrs Jepson.' He looked at Lady Allenby. 'I don't know how to say this in any other way, Lady Allenby, so I'll come straight out with it, and hope that you will not be too embarrassed. She wanted me to make love to her – she even took off her dress – and she *begged* me to make love. She said she was very lonely, that her husband was old and that he was not very well, and I became more and more alarmed. I told her that all I wanted was for her to leave me alone. I said I was going up on deck and that I hoped she would be gone before I returned.'

The Chairman and Lady Allenby were speechless.

Andrew went on: 'Mrs Jepson threatened to come to my cabin every night and she said that if I ever told anyone she would deny it. She said that her story would be that I had tried to rape her and that she had come to my cabin because I had invited her.' He paused. 'When I got back to my cabin, Mrs Jepson had gone, but she had left this behind.' Andrew gave Sir Colin the note and the ten thousand dollar cheque. Lady Allenby and he read it together. When they had finished Andrew said, 'I don't know what on earth to do. Can you please advise me? I didn't know who to turn to for help.'

Lady Allenby was the first to move. She leant forward and put a hand on Andrew's knee. 'Poor Andrew, how awful for you. I never did like that woman. She's sailed with us before, you know.'

Sir Colin asked, 'Does Sarah know anything about this?'

'No, sir, she doesn't,' Andrew replied.

'I think we should tell her, Andrew. You see, if Mrs Jepson goes to Sarah first, Sarah might find it hard to know who to believe. However, if we tell Sarah now, just as you've told us, and show her the letter and the cheque, she'll know at once that you are not to blame and that you are not involved in any way.' Sir Colin went on: 'How old are you, Andrew?'

'Twenty-three, sir.'

'Well, for twenty-three I think you've handled this nasty little drama very well. You've done the right thing in coming to me and I'll be very glad to help you in any way I can. I'll keep this note and the cheque for the time being, and we'll play any future developments by ear. However, don't tell Mrs Jepson that you've come to me. Let her think you still have the cheque. I think Sarah is sunbathing,' he turned to his wife. 'We ought to tell her now, don't you think?' He got to his feet.

'Yes, I do,' said Lady Allenby, and she put her arm through Andrew's. 'We're on your side, Andrew; we'll sort this out for you. Just keep us posted on developments. Poor you! What a way to start a voyage.'

Andrew was sitting at a desk in the ship's library, writing to his parents, when Sarah found him. He stood up.

'Oh, Andrew, how awful for you. I had a horrible feeling last night that that dreadful woman was up to something. I'm so glad you've told my father everything. Can we have a drink together before lunch?'

'Of course. Let's go to the swimming pool bar.'

When they got to the bar, Sarah ordered a tomato juice and Andrew asked for a beer. She said, 'You can like it or not, Andy, but I'm going to stick pretty close to you until my father has sorted out the dreaded Mrs J!'

'I hope you will. I'd love you to stick closely to me. I hope you won't find it boring.'

'You silly boy – if I do find it boring, I'll cast you to La Jepson!'

At lunch, Cynthia Jepson still stared at Andrew quite a lot, almost looking for a reaction from him. Sarah had the feeling that Mrs Jepson was feeling pretty confident, and was in no way abashed at what had happened in Andrew's cabin the previous night.

The afternoon, evening and dinner passed without undue excitement. It was just after eleven o'clock that night, and Andrew was already in bed, reading, when the door opened suddenly and Cynthia Jepson came straight in. She closed the door, lay on top of Andrew and started kissing him hungrily – he had never before experienced such passion. When he tried to get free she pinned him down fiercely and pleaded with him. 'Don't send me away, Andrew, please. Let me just stay for an hour and I'll go away quietly. Please, Andrew. I need you so badly.'

Andrew managed to get free and stood up. 'I told you last night that you were not to come to my cabin. I don't want you here. I don't want to have anything to do with you. Please go!'

Her mood changed from pleading. Far from going, the lady stood up and calmly undressed. She was naked from head to foot and she walked up to Andrew. 'Take your pyjamas off and come here,' she commanded. 'Come on, take your pyjamas off!'

'I'll do no such thing. I'm going to put my dressing gown on and I'm going up on deck.'

Cynthia Jepson walked slowly to the bed and lay down. 'Oh no you're not,' she said, 'and I'll tell you why. You make one move towards that door and I'll press this bell for your night steward. He'll come in and see me naked. I wonder what he'll think? In case he thinks you're just going to go to bed with me I'll scream and shout, and say you've been trying to rape me. Don't get me wrong, I'll tear those pyjamas off before the steward knocks on the door, and you'll have blood on you, see these nails? They'll produce the blood for me and you.' She put a finger on the bell. 'Go on – try and go on deck.'

Andrew hesitated. She calmed down. 'There's a good boy – now come and give me the sort of love I've paid you ten thousand dollars for, and I don't mean only tonight – I mean every night until you leave the ship at Colombo.'

Andrew stared at the woman for a moment. 'I'll call your bluff,' he said. He put on his dressing gown and left.

'You bloody little shit!' muttered Cynthia to herself.

At breakfast the next morning the Jepsons had not appeared and Sir Colin leant towards Andrew and said very softly, 'Did you have some more drama with our lady-friend last night, Andrew?'

'Yes, I certainly did, sir – how did you know?'

'The Purser rang me in our cabin half an hour ago. It seems that Mrs Jepson has laid a very serious charge against you. She says that you persuaded her to come to your cabin last night and that you tried to rape her. She says she has scratches and bruises to prove it. I know this can't be true, Andrew?'

'No, sir, that accusation isn't true. Yes, it *is* true that she came to my cabin last night, about eleven o'clock, after I was in bed, and again she pleaded with me to make love to her.' He looked at Sarah and her mother. 'Please believe me, Lady Allenby, and you Sarah.

She said something to the effect that she wanted value for the ten thousand dollars she had paid me. She also said she proposed to come to my cabin every night until we reached Colombo. She went on to say that if I didn't take my pyjamas off at once and go to bed with her she'd ring for the night steward and yell and scream and tell him I'd tried to rape her. I didn't know what on earth to do, and then I decided to call her bluff, although I wasn't at all sure if she was bluffing. Anyway, I went out and on to a lower deck and, when I came back, she had gone.'

'That's the whole story, the true story, Andrew?' asked Sir Colin.

'Absolutely true, sir, no exaggeration. I can't take much more of this.'

'I hope you won't have to. I've asked the Purser to ask the Jepsons to come with him to our private drawing room at ten o'clock. I doubt very much if Mr Jepson will come; he probably knows nothing of all this. Anyway Andrew, I want you to be there too. Please say very little, just answer my questions. I want Mrs Jepson to feel that she's got you where she wants you. You'll have to trust me.'

'Of course I'll trust you, sir. I'm so grateful I've got someone like you on my side. I'll be at your drawing room door just before ten.' He turned to Sarah 'Please believe me.'

To Lady Allenby's amusement, and approval, Sarah put her hand on Andrew's and squeezed it. 'Of course I believe you – Mum and I will be in the next cabin and, with the door open, we shall listen in to the whole drama. I don't know how my father proposes to handle this, but you can be sure it'll be good. Poor Andy, I feel so sorry for you. That wretched woman!'

Andrew knocked at the door to the Allenby's suite at five minutes to ten, and Sir Colin let him in. There was a small hall which led to a handsomely appointed drawing room, with French doors leading onto a private deck. 'Come in, Andrew, and don't worry. Leave things to me, and only answer specific questions, unless I ask you to describe something in detail. Stand over there, would you?'

'Good luck, Andy,' whispered Sarah, poking her head round her parents' bedroom door.

Andrew had only been standing by the French windows for a few moments, staring out to sea, when there was a knock on the door. The Allenby's steward answered it and stood aside while Mrs Jepson, followed by the Captain and the Purser, entered. She put a hand to her mouth in surprise when she saw Andrew.

As he walked forward to meet the party Sir Colin, who had seen Mrs Jepson's little gesture of surprise, thought to himself, *Good, first point to us. She didn't expect Andrew to be present.* He settled the visitors and left Andrew standing by the French doors, still staring out to sea. Lady Allenby and Sarah were well within hearing distance in the Allenby's bedroom.

The steward arrived with coffee and, after he had served the party and left, Sir Colin turned to Mrs Jepson.

'Mrs Jepson, as Chairman of the Company, I must offer you my apologies for the very unpleasant experience you had last night. The Purser has told me what happened and, let me assure you, I fully understand your distress. This is not the sort of thing we like to happen on our ships.'

Mrs Jepson's relief was clear to see. She had recovered from the shock of seeing Andrew, and Sir Colin's reassuring remarks acted like a tonic.

Sir Colin went on: 'Now, I've had an account of last night's unpleasantness from the Purser. It's important that I hear the whole story, in detail, from you, Mrs Jepson, so that I shall then know how to deal with Mr Harvey. Don't hurry – just tell me the whole story in your own words and in your own time and don't leave anything out. I want the case against Mr Harvey to be complete and watertight.'

Mrs Jepson couldn't believe her ears. There was no doubt, she felt, that things were going her way.

'Well, after dinner last night,' she said, 'my husband went to bed rather early. He's not very strong, you know, and he's not too well. I went back to the main lounge for coffee when Mr Harvey came up to me and sat down. We chatted for some time and I must admit I enjoyed our little session. Mr Harvey was very complimentary and he flattered me a lot. I asked him if he was comfortable on board and he said he was, although his cabin was rather small. "Why don't you come and look at it?" he said. Here, I must admit, Sir Colin, I was very foolish. I'm old enough to have known better. I had had quite a lot to drink at dinner and, feeling pleasantly flattered by Mr Harvey's remarks, saw no harm in accepting his invitation to look at his cabin. I fell for the oldest trick in the book, Sir Colin; instead of going to look at his etchings, I went to look at his cabin. We went in and Mr Harvey's mood changed suddenly. He became like a maniac. He started tearing at my clothes, and threw me down on the bed. He is very strong, and in tearing off my panties he bruised and scratched me badly. I can show you if you like?'

Sir Colin held up a hand and shook his head. 'Go on, Mrs Jepson,' he invited.

'Well, I couldn't reach the bell to ring for help, but I managed to get free and tried to get out of the cabin. Mr Harvey caught me at the door and said, "You can't escape. I'm going to make love to you whether you like it or not. It's no good struggling; you'll only make it worse for yourself." I could see he was right and so I started pleading with him. I said I would give him money if he would let me go. The talk of money seemed to work and, still holding me against the door he said, "How much?" I said "Five thousand, ten thousand dollars, anything!" He let me go but the door was locked and then Mr Harvey said, "You must do more than that. Not only must you give me ten thousand dollars, you must write me a little note saying you wanted this to happen and that you are giving me a present so that I will make love to you all through the voyage." I had my cheque book in my purse and so I gave him his money and the note he wanted. Then he allowed me to go back to my cabin, where my husband was fast asleep. I had a shower and tried to sleep, but I couldn't. I reported all this to the Purser this morning.'

She sat back, put a little handkerchief to her eyes, and tried to look pathetic. She was very pleased with her story. She knew the Chairman, the Captain and the Purser were all on her side and finally it would be Harvey's word against hers. There would be no contest.

Andrew was horrified at the tissue of lies he had just heard but he was worried that it all sounded so plausible, so genuine. Lady Allenby and Sarah were also having some doubts.

Sir Colin said nothing for a moment or two. He leant forward. 'Mrs Jepson, I'm horrified at what you've just told us all and I'm taking the most serious view of the terrible drama you have described which happened last night. The matter is so important that I must first clear up one or two points before I tackle Mr Harvey. I must be in no doubt whatever on any point before I charge Mr Harvey and decide what I'm going to do with him.' He turned towards Andrew's back. 'I'm disgusted with you, Mr Harvey, and my wife and daughter will be equally disgusted when they hear about this. You will not be sitting at our table again; in fact, I'll probably have you put ashore at Gibraltar.' He turned to Cynthia Jepson. 'Now, first, let's get the date and time right, Mr Harvey invited you to his cabin last night?'

'Yes, last night.'

'And he assaulted you last night, a few hours ago? Perhaps eleven or twelve hours ago?'

'Yes, that's right.'

'You're in no doubt about the date and time, Mrs Jepson? You see, if this matter goes to the police, and I think it will, they will want to be perfectly sure when it all happened. So we must get it straight.'

Cynthia Jepson wanted to burst out laughing. This was all too easy. She would have given anything to see Andrew's face. She replied, 'It was last night, a few hours ago. It seems like it was only a few moments ago, it was so horrifying!'

'Well, I must apologise to you once more, Mrs Jepson. And more than that, I'll be sending a report to my colleagues in London suggesting some form of compensation for you to make some amends for Mr Harvey's shameful behaviour. You've given me all the facts, the true facts? You are quite sure?'

Sarah looked at her mother in the next door cabin. She was on the verge of tears. 'Dad's fallen for it, Mum!' she sobbed. 'Andrew's innocent, I know he is. I can't believe the way Dad is acting.' Lady Allenby tried to console her daughter but she was equally alarmed.

Sir Colin repeated his question: 'You are quite sure these are all the true facts, Mrs Jepson?'

'Yes, yes, yes!' she said.

Sir Colin got to his feet and stood in front of Mrs Jepson. 'If all you've told me is true, Mrs Jepson, that is to say that Mr Harvey attacked you last night, a few hours ago, how is it that he brought and gave me your cheque and your note yesterday morning and your cheque has the date of the *day before that*? You've just told me a pack of lies, Mrs Jepson. I don't believe a word of what you've just said. Mr Harvey saw me at eleven o'clock yesterday morning and told me how you entered his cabin, the night before last, and demanded sex. I believe Mr Harvey.

Mrs Jepson had gone quite white.

Sir Colin went on: 'I'll give you two choices, Mrs Jepson. We're calling, very briefly, at Gibraltar the day after tomorrow and your first choice is that we put you and your husband ashore there – we'll refund your whole passage money. Your second choice is that we have the police on board and I'll lay charges against you. Here is your cheque. Mr Harvey has told me that he wouldn't touch it even if it was for a million dollars. Please let me know by this evening what you want to do.' He walked to a bell and when the steward entered, said, 'Please show Mrs Jepson to her cabin, Carter.'

The Jepsons opted to be put ashore at Gibraltar. The Purser put them at another table for their few remaining meals, in order to avoid embarrassment.

From a secluded corner of the rail Andrew watched the Jepsons go ashore with their luggage. His relief at seeing them go was mixed with gratitude to Sir Colin for the quite brilliant way he had handled the interview. Before he had left the Chairman's suite he had thanked Sir Colin for his kindness and for the clever trap he had set for Mrs Jepson. 'I'm only thankful you came to me yesterday morning with her letter and her cheque,' said Sir Colin. 'I think had you not done so, you would have had an uncomfortable voyage to Colombo!'

Chapter 2

Just before lunch, as the ship was preparing to sail, Andrew saw Sarah staring at the great Rock of Gibraltar. He joined her and she gave him a little peck on the cheek. She was looking very pretty and relaxed, and Andrew longed to put his arm round her, but refrained. Sarah pointed to the Rock. 'Have you ever seen that before, Andy?' He shook his head and she said, 'I have, and I went ashore here two years ago. Did you know that the Rock is swarming with Barbary Apes? They're quite big and visitors have to be careful because the apes are rather bold and may attack you if you annoy them. Sometimes they attack you anyway. There's a superstition here that if the apes ever leave the Rock, it will fall to an invasion by Spain. Rather like the ravens leaving the Tower of London.'

'Yes, I had heard that about the apes, Sarah. Changing the subject, I must say that your father was marvellous the day before yesterday. I don't know how I can ever thank him. I shudder to think what would have happened had I not had him to turn to.'

'Mum and I were very proud of Dad – but, at the beginning, he seemed to be so much on that awful woman's side that we were beginning to get seriously worried.'

'Yes, I felt that too – but then I remembered he had told me to say nothing and to trust him – then I knew everything would be OK. It was his words "to trust me" that did the trick.'

As the ship sailed away from Gibraltar and into the Mediterranean the whole atmosphere seemed to change. The sea was a deep, almost unbelievable, blue, and the sun felt hotter. The air took on a different scent – it was spicy and very different to the Atlantic of only a day or so before. Romance was in the air, too.

Sarah and Andrew saw a lot of each other and her parents became very attached to this eligible young bachelor of whom their daughter seemed so fond.

It was a busy life on board: early morning swims, deck games, very leisurely afternoons and quite glamorous and entertaining evenings.

A number of the younger ship's officers could usually be seen on the boat deck, after dinner, with some pretty young thing in tow. The lifeboats offered enough privacy for young couples to hide between them and the rails.

One morning Sarah asked Andrew if he had ever put any money on the ship's tote.

He replied, 'I watch people going into the tavern bar every day before lunch and staring at a blackboard with figures on it but I've no idea what it's all about, apart from the fact that it has something to do with betting.'

'It *is* a sort of gamble,' said Sarah. 'The ship does so many miles every twenty-four hours and passengers try to guess exactly how many miles she covers. The Captain gives an approximate figure, usually between four hundred and fifty and five hundred miles, depending on the weather, and you have to guess the right figure. At twelve noon precisely the ship sounds its siren and the ship's log is read. This gives the exact mileage, and if you've bet on the right figure you get the money in the kitty – or else you may have to share it with other winners who've got the same figure.'

'How much do you bet?'

'Everyone pays half-a-crown, and the winner usually collects eight or nine pounds, but that depends on how many people have bet.'

'What's the time?' asked Andrew.

Sarah looked at her watch 'You've got twenty minutes to lose half-a-crown!'

'If I do I'll have to go without my morning beer,' said Andrew.

The ship's course was east-south-east and she passed between Tunis, on the North African coast, and to the South of Sicily heading for Port Said at the mouth of the Suez Canal. The weather grew warmer every day and Andrew revelled in the wonderfully new experience of a long sea voyage.

The night before the ship anchored at Port Said, Sarah and Andrew were on the boat deck after dinner. The moon was full and some lights could be seen far away on the Egyptian coastline. Sarah looked radiant and Andrew could smell her perfume and the soft and intriguing scent of her hair. He put his arm through hers and they kissed. 'Sarah darling – I must talk to you.'

She turned her head quickly and looked at him with a puzzled frown. 'Is there something wrong, Andy?'

'In a way, yes – something horribly wrong.'

Sarah gripped his hand tightly. 'Andy, what is it? I couldn't bear it if you had something awful to tell me. What is it?'

He put his arms round her and drew her close to him. 'It's this. I've fallen in love with you, Sarah darling . . .'

This was as far as he got. Sarah grabbed him and pulled his head down and kissed him savagely. As she broke away, she whispered, 'Is falling in love with me so "horribly wrong"?'

Andrew led Sarah to a wooden seat by the side of a ventilator. He held her hand. 'My darling, as you know, I'm going out to Ceylon to become a tea planter, and I've had to sign an agreement with the Tea Company who are employing me. This agreement is for five years which means I don't see England again during that time. That's not all that bad; what *is* bad is that I'm not allowed to marry in my first agreement. I was going to ask you in a few days' time if you cared for me, then I suddenly remembered this clause in my agreement which says I can't marry for five years. If you had said that you did care for me – enough, perhaps, to marry me – I would have gone to your parents to tell them how I felt. Now that's impossible. I couldn't possibly ask you to wait five years; it wouldn't be fair.'

Sarah looked away. 'Have you got a handkerchief?' She dabbed her eyes which had suddenly become wet with emotion. 'Andy, darling, I love you too, and I don't think five years is all that long – is it?'

'I'm so very glad you've said you love me. I'll remember that all my life. It's the most precious thing. But I'm not going to ask you to marry me, Sarah darling, because, well, as I say, it wouldn't be fair on you. I've thought it all out. It's that we would not be able to see each other. We might be able to meet once or twice in five years if your father would give you a passage on one of his ships. Even that would take you three or four weeks. You're young, you're very lovely, you have the sweetest nature and I wish to goodness I had met you in England before I took up this planting job.'

'Let's talk in the morning,' said Sarah. 'I can't stand any more of this tonight, it's too awful. Goodnight, my darling.'

Andrew watched her go down the companionway to the deck below. He followed soon after and stood by the rail staring at the moonlit sea wondering what would happen. He hated the thought that perhaps he had hurt Sarah, but somehow he felt he had done the right thing. He went to his cabin and finally fell into a fitful asleep.

Two things woke him early the following morning. Firstly, he felt and heard the engines stop; then, because his porthole was wide open, he heard a strange babble of voices from below. He looked down and saw the ship had laid anchor. The shore was only a hundred yards or so away and he saw one very big shop and several smaller ones. There seemed to be palm trees everywhere.

The noise that woke Andrew came from the fleet of small boats surrounding the ship. These were filled with shouting and gesticulating Egyptians offering their wares for sale to the passengers lining the rails. It was a wonderfully colourful scene in the brilliant early morning sunlight.

The swimming pool was closed while the ship was in port, so Andrew had a quick bath and went on deck. Some of the passengers had already gone down to breakfast and he found a gap in the rails and looked down. He was spotted at once by one of the vendors.

'Hallo, Mr MacTavish, you buy this fine leather pouffe, very good for resting the foots. Made of real camel skin. Mrs MacTavish very pleased you buy. Come along, Mr MacTavish, you buy, if not for Mrs MacTavish then for your girlfriend Miss MacSporran, hey, toots mon, just a few bawbees, you look – you buy.'

Andrew turned away and wondered whether he dared face Sarah at breakfast. His problem was solved by seeing her walking towards him. She put an arm through his.

'I hardly slept a wink last night, Andy. What about you?'

'Not much, I was too sad.'

'I had a lot of time to think and this is what I feel we ought to do,' said Sarah. She went on: 'First, I'm so glad you love me and, as I said last night, I love you too. Let's always keep that as a treasured memory. I think we must wait for your five years to be over; I don't think we can avoid that, but let's go on loving each other and let events take their course. Let's write to each other regularly and let's both understand, quite clearly, that if one or other of us meets someone else, then there are to be no hard feelings.'

Andrew was silent, digesting what Sarah had said. 'I think you're absolutely right – there seems to be no alternative.' He kissed her on the cheek. 'You're very clever to have thought everything out so clearly – it's far more than I could have done. I didn't even know what on earth I was going to say to you this morning.'

'I can't take all the credit, Andy. When the steward took Mum and Dad's early-morning tea into their cabin I went in too. I told them everything. They were sweet. Dad thinks you've been very brave and straightforward, and Mum said we should just leave things as they are and see what happens. They both said that it was pathetically obvious that we were in love and they both agreed that they liked the prospect. Then Mum said that five years was a long time to be apart and that, with the best will in the world, it would be unfair if one expected the other not to change, or meet someone else, in that time. So Andy darling, let's go on being in love, let's have a wonderful voyage and, when we reach Colombo, we say *Au revoir*, not goodbye.'

They decided to skip breakfast and they moved to the rail where the hawkers below were still in full cry. 'They call them "bum" boats,' said Sarah, 'but don't ask me why.'

Sarah and Andrew were spotted at once from below 'Hey there, Mrs MacSporran, you buy these nice pearls, real pearls, this necklace worn by Queen Nefetiti when she building the Pyramids! You buy, only two pounds, real pearls!'

'Why all these Scottish names?' asked Andrew.

'I've no idea, they've always done it. I think it's very funny.'

They were joined at the rail by Sir Colin and Lady Allenby. They both took in the view for a moment, then Lady Allenby put her arm through Andrew's. 'I'm so sorry that you and Sarah have this sadness, Andrew. She's told us all about it, and my husband and I feel for you both. We think if you let events take their course it will be fairest for both Sarah and yourself.' She squeezed his arm.

'There's no alternative, I know,' said Andrew, 'but I hope it may be possible for Sarah to visit me in Ceylon, perhaps once or twice, during my first five year agreement.'

Apparently changing the subject, Sir Colin asked, 'Have you ever heard of the Gulli Gulli man, Andrew?'

'No, sir. Who's he?'

'Well, he's an Egyptian who comes on board and does the most marvellous tricks for the passengers. He makes baby chicks appear out of nowhere, out of little girls' noses, out of your ear. He's quite marvellous. He does hundreds of tricks. It says on the notice-board that he's coming on board at eleven. We must watch him.'

They had good seats round the open-air dance floor and, as Sir Colin had said, the Gulli Gulli man was astonishing. After making all sorts of things appear and disappear, he started to wind up his show. 'Ladies and gentlemen, this is my last trick, very good trick. Will some lady give me her best and most beautiful diamond ring? You Mrs MacGregor, that is a fine ring. You give me that.'

'No way!' said 'Mrs MacGregor'.

'Then you, Mrs MacKenzie, you buy that ring in your Woolworths, no?'

In fact it was 'Mrs MacKenzie's' engagement ring and consisted of a lovely emerald surrounded by diamonds. Reluctantly she handed it over. The Gulli Gulli man produced a breakfast roll and broke it, placing the ring inside and, holding the roll firmly, said, 'Now, ladies and gentlemen, I am a poor man and my young boy here will take round my hat and will you please put some money in it.'

People were quite generous and, while his fez was going round, he started packing up. He went on: 'Now for my famous trick with Mrs MacKenzie's ring!' He picked up the roll, opened it and showed the ring inside to the passengers.

'Now this trick needs three magic words, you must all shout out, "Goodbye, goodbye, goodbye.'

All the passengers shouted 'Goodbye' and the Gulli Gulli man walked to the rail and hurled the roll over the side and into the sea. They all saw it go.

'And now *I* say goodbye!' He started to depart.

'But where's my ring?' screamed 'Mrs MacKenzie' and her husband looked menacing.

'What ring?' asked the Gulli Gulli man innocently.

'You know damn well,' shouted 'Mr MacKenzie', 'it's my wife's engagement ring.'

'Oh, *that* ring. Why it's here all the time!' He walked over to 'Mr MacKenzie' and, in full view of the astonished passengers, he produced the ring from 'Mr MacKenzie's' nose! The passengers all clapped enthusiastically.

As the passengers started to disperse, Sir Colin turned to Andrew. 'We're lunching ashore at a hotel with the P & 0 Agents, Andrew – would you like to join us?'

Andrew glanced at Sarah, who nodded vigorously.

'I'd love to, sir. Thank you very much.'

'And you and I can shop and explore Port Said afterwards,' said Sarah.

Sarah and Andrew were both understandably quiet at first but, once ashore, there was so much to occupy them that they forgot, temporarily, the sadness in their hearts.

Lunch was quite different to anything Andrew had experienced before. There was a lot of marble in the hotel, and green palms in stone tubs were everywhere. The servants were clad in white and this contrasted sharply with their red fezzes or tarbooshes. The party had drinks under fans in a cool, marble-pillared hall before moving into lunch.

Sir Colin complemented and thanked his host for providing French wines.

'I didn't think Lady Allenby would care for the local stuff,' said his host, and he went on: 'I drank quite a lot at a party one evening and my mouth the next morning tasted, if you'll forgive the expression, like a camel driver's sock!'

'How disgusting,' said Sarah, but Sir Colin and Andrew loved the description.

The party split up after lunch and Sarah took Andrew shopping. 'You'd better buy a sunhat or topee, Andrew,' said Sir Colin. 'Sarah knows where you can get one.'

Sarah did indeed know, and they walked to Simon Artz, a sort of 'Harrods' of Port Said. The snag about walking was the constant pestering they had from street vendors who offered them anything from 'feelthy pos'cards' to addresses where Andrew could discover the delights some Port Said ladies had on offer. They decided on walking because they both felt sorry for the pathetically thin horses that were pulling the carriages for hire.

Andrew found a sunhat which suited him and delighted Sarah. 'You look so dashing, darling,' she beamed and, on looking in a full-length mirror, he too was pleased with the adornment on his six foot three frame. He hoped they wore them in Ceylon. Sarah bought some Turkish Delight which seemed a strange thing to buy in Egypt, but it was being sold everywhere. Simon Artz was a wonderful shop and the young couple spent a happy hour browsing.

As the evening ferry was taking passengers back to the ship, which was not due to sail until midnight, Andrew noticed a crowd standing at the ship's rail looking upwards. This puzzled him until he reached the pontoon by the side of the liner. Someone pointed upwards and both Sarah and he saw some small Egyptian boys, almost naked, balancing themselves on a rail by the ship's wing bridge. This must have been some sixty or seventy feet above the water. A passenger on the boat deck threw a coin in the air and just before it touched the sea a small naked boy dived. He seemed to be in the air a long, long time but he splashed down only a second or so after the coin. A few moments later he appeared on the surface with the silver coin in his mouth. He waved this to the passengers, saluted and started his swim back to the dock. The other four or five little boys all did the same trick. It was a marvellous exhibition of showmanship.

After dinner Andrew said he would like to go ashore again. Sarah looked doubtful but Sir Colin put his hand on her arm and said to

Andrew, 'You'll both be quite all right so long as you keep to the main, well-lit, roads. Don't go down any dark alleys. And don't forget we sail at midnight, so be back on board in good time.'

The couple strolled arm-in-arm and Andrew was fascinated with all that he saw. They were still pestered to some extent by hawkers and pimps, but Andrew felt more confident in dealing with them now. They passed a nice-looking hotel which advertised that there would be a belly-dancer performing there at ten o'clock.

Sarah tugged on Andrew's arm. 'Come on, Andy – let's go in and have a drink and watch the woman!'

They found a table for two and Andrew ordered drinks. The belly-dancer appeared sharp on ten. She wore a jewel-encrusted bra and transparent gauze baggy trousers which ended above her ankles which were adorned with bracelets and little bells. Her navel, in full view, had a large glittering gem stuck in it. She was certainly attractive and it was by no means her first ever appearance as a belly-dancer. Sarah watched Andrew's reaction with amusement until the dancer spotted this handsome young giant and came across to their table and danced about a foot away from him. He was torn between embarrassment and admiration, but did what was expected of him. He produced a note and handed it to the girl. She kissed the top of his head, gave him a bewitching smile, stuffed the note into her practically non-existent bra and wriggled off.

'I'm not bringing you here again, you seducer!' hissed Sarah trying to look cross.

'I didn't do a thing!' said Andrew, feeling very pleased with himself. 'Let's have another drink.'

'Oh no you don't,' said Sarah. 'I'm not having you falling for a belly-dancer. I'm taking you back to the ship, my lad! Actually, you looked so sweet when she was dancing for you. I wanted to kiss you myself!'

Andrew woke as usual the next morning when his steward brought him his early-morning tea. He noticed that the engine's vibration was less than usual and he walked over to his porthole and looked out. To his astonishment he saw an Arab on a camel a hundred yards away. He was leading another camel. There was nothing but desert in the background. Andrew suddenly realised that they were in the Suez Canal. He dressed hurriedly and went up on deck and found a vantage point by the rail overlooking the bows of the ship. An arm gently slid through his.

'Good morning, Casanova!' said Sarah.

'Good morning, my love. Isn't this super?' Andrew exclaimed holding her hand. 'I'd no idea the Canal was so narrow!'

'Yes – they have to have special stretches where two ships can pass each other. Because of this there are a number of lakes along the Canal where ships have to tie up and wait until the narrow bit is empty.'

'How long will we be in the Canal?' asked Andrew.

'Most of the day – it's about a hundred miles long, I think. The real time to do it is at night, with a full moon, on the boat deck. Very romantic!'

Andrew turned to her. 'I do love you so, Sarah darling. Last night I even thought about chucking up this planting job and going back to England. That idea didn't last long. I realised I'd be out of a job, and without any money, and so I'd be no nearer to proposing to you than I am now.'

They stood at the forward rail in silence.

'We must not rush this, Andy – we decided we wouldn't. I'm convinced that after a few years – horrible, sad years – we'll be together for good. Anyway, that's my target but I can't possibly achieve it without your help.'

'You talk about *my* help – it's *your* help that's going to be the strong one, the dependable one. That's what's going to keep me going for the next five years. I'll wait for you, my darling.'

'You better had! Now come on, we're supposed to be enjoying the Suez Canal! Some people call it the "Sewage" Canal because the locals do some nasty things in it!'

Sarah's cheerfulness did Andrew's spirits a lot of good. 'Right, let's have some breakfast and come back on deck. I've never seen anything like this in my life.'

After breakfast the young couple found chairs in the swimming pool area. Chairs proved to be the wrong choice because as soon as they settled down to watch something across the starboard beam, something more exciting happened to port. They finished up by leaning against whichever rail offered the best entertainment.

Andrew, as he had said, had never seen anything like the Suez Canal. It kept him fascinated, and nearly everyone remarked on how little work was being done on the banks. There were gangs of Egyptian labourers everywhere but few signs of activity. The morning was hot, admittedly, but nearly all the workmen were spreadeagled on the desert sand staring at the ship. One wag remarked that they should call the non-activity 'Egyptian P.T.', for which he said the word of command should be 'On the backs down – and remain!'

The ship didn't stop at Suez at the south end of the Canal but steamed through the Gulf of Suez and into the Red Sea. The weather was very hot indeed, and Andrew saw his first flying fish. Their silvery bodies and 'wings' were clearly seen as they left the water and planed above the surface for ten or twenty yards before they returned to the sea with a little splash. There were a lot of porpoises, too, leaping out of the water and managing to keep up with the speed of the ship.

At dinner that evening Sarah turned towards Andrew and lowered her voice. 'Keep this to yourself, Andy, because the Captain doesn't want the passengers to know.'

'What is it – what's happened?' asked Andrew.

'A steward died early this morning. The ship's doctor says it's sunstroke. This was the steward's first voyage – he's quite a young man and he had no idea how hot the sun is here. He was apparently glued to the rail over the stern of the ship, with no hat on, for most of the canal. He then collapsed and died. They're going to bury him at sea before dawn – it's the usual custom. You'll notice the engines stopping and, if you're interested, go down to the lowest deck near the stern and watch.'

The following morning Andrew woke up as soon as the engines had stopped. He did as Sarah said and found a small party of sailors assembled, together with the Captain. The dead steward had been sewn into a canvas coffin and his body was placed on a wide polished plank. The Captain said a prayer and the sailors lifted the plank towards a gap in the rails and tilted it towards the sea. Without a sound the canvas-covered body slid into the sea, making only a small splash as it hit the water. The Captain threw a wreath gently over the side and the engines started at once. Andrew was very moved by the simple dignity of the burial and walked slowly back to his cabin.

A few days later, early in the morning, the liner steamed into Aden harbour. The gaunt barren rocks towered over the port and one could be forgiven for wondering if any life existed in such a hostile-looking place. In fact life existed very much, as Sir Colin explained to Andrew.

'It's a thriving place, Andrew, and, although it looks forbidding and inhospitable, would you believe that young men of your age clamour to be sent here. The reason is that life is very social in Aden and expatriates thoroughly enjoy themselves swimming, sailing, playing tennis and, of course, there's the inevitable round of parties in the evening. However' – Sir Colin went on – 'the main reason for Aden's popularity with the young men from Britain is because it's regarded as a "hardship" posting and all employees from abroad get a special "hardship" allowance. Very often this is so generous that people can live quite happily on this allowance and not touch their salaries which are salted away in England. I know all this for a fact, because we treat the people in our Agents' office here in the same way.'

Andrew wondered whether he would be better off as a Steamer Agent in Aden rather than a tea planter in Ceylon. *Too late to change now*, he thought.

The young couple went ashore and were pestered as usual by the Arab shopkeepers and pavement hawkers. One man was most persistent. 'Come and see mermaids, very rare sight, must see mermaids.' Sarah sent him away by saying she had seen the 'mermaids' several times before and they were awful!

'What are these mermaids?' asked Andrew.

'They're sort of sea mammals called "Dugongs", I believe. They're quite hideous, fat and bloated, and they say mermaids originated from them and I find that hard to believe. They're in a museum.'

'You really are the little walking encyclopaedia aren't you, darling. You make me feel like the village idiot!'

'Andy, I've done this voyage more than once, I *should* know a thing or two about these places.'

It was extremely hot in Aden and the couple had a drink in a hotel and decided to go back on board for lunch. Sir Colin and Lady Allenby had friends from Aden to entertain on board and so Andrew and Sarah had a salad on deck.

In the afternoon Sarah turned to Andrew. They were in their swimming costumes, in the shade, lying almost flat in deck chairs. She held out her hand and he took it. 'If we were married, Andy, I know what I'd like to do now.'

Andrew sighed. 'This must be telepathy, or whatever they call it. I've been thinking exactly the same thing. All I can think of at the moment is how much I'd give to be able to make love to you. You look so adorable, you *are* adorable, I was wondering if we could creep down to my cabin quietly, the ship's practically empty and, er, have a rest, so to speak, on my bunk.' He waited in trepidation for Sarah's reaction. He didn't have long to wait. She was out of her chair in a flash, gathering her things together.

'Lead on, MacDuff,' she smiled 'Your faithful concubine is close behind you.'

They arrived unseen and Andrew locked the cabin door and closed the shutters over the porthole. There was a dull, greenish light in the cabin. Sarah turned back the bed cover and slipped out of her bathing suit. Andrew just stood and stared. He'd never seen anything so lovely, so desirable. He took off his swimming trunks, watching Sarah while she lay down. He knelt by the bunk and kissed her. 'I want you Sarah, darling, as I've never wanted anything in my life before. Yet, I'd never forgive myself if I allowed myself to go all the way with you now. Am I very dull and old-fashioned?'

'Stand up – let me see you.'

He stood.

'Wow! There's nothing dull or old-fashioned about you, my darling. I've never done this before, and I'm almost out of my mind to do it now, but you're right, of course. Let's just play with each other for now and, one day, with clear consciences, I'll beg you to make love to me properly.'

They lay together, kissing passionately. Sarah's hand strayed down towards Andrew's groin. His did the same to Sarah, and for a while they enjoyed touching and caressing each other's bodies, each bringing the other to the peak of excitement.

Afterwards, feeling relaxed, the young couple slept for half an hour in each other's arms.

The ship sailed that night and started her long journey to Colombo. The hot, sunny days were taken up with deck games and, in the evenings there was dancing, or the movies, or bridge.

One morning at breakfast the Captain told his party that they would be passing a sister ship at about eleven o'clock, and that it was quite an exciting event. He asked Sir Colin if he would like to bring four or five guests to the port wing bridge to watch. The other ship came in sight just before eleven and seemed to be almost on a collision course. Both ships were doing over twenty knots and so the distance between them was closing rapidly. Almost at a given signal, both vessels blew their sirens, which made everyone jump, and the coxswains put their helms hard over to starboard so that they crossed with only a hundred yards or so between them. It was all very thrilling.

The day before they were due in at Colombo, Sir Colin told Andrew that he was having a private lunch party on board the next day because it was the ship's maiden voyage. He said the Governor of Ceylon, his wife, and some members of his staff would be there, and so would the senior partners of the ship's Agents in Colombo. Sir Colin said they would be delighted if Andrew would come too as a sort of farewell present.

Andrew said there would be nothing he would like more, but he would be leaving the ship before lunch. He explained: 'The Tea Company I'm going to work for have Agents in Colombo and they are coming on board to collect me at ten o'clock, and then take me to their office.'

It was a lovely clear morning as the ship neared the island and Andrew and Sarah had got up very early to watch. The sea was like a sheet of dark blue glass. They held hands and were feeling sad, both dreading the moment when they knew they would have to part for such a long time.

The officer of the watch spoke over the tannoy. 'If you look over the port bow you will see a triangular-shaped peak on the horizon. It is the famous Adam's Peak, a holy mountain, and it is some eighty or ninety miles away. Legend has it that the Lord Buddha left his footprint on the Peak and thousands of pilgrims climb to the summit every year to worship. If you now look over the starboard quarter you can see some whales on the surface about a mile away. They blow every few moments.'

The young couple saw the Pilot come alongside and ascend to the bridge. The great ship slipped slowly through the harbour entrance with its port and starboard lighthouses marking the channel. Two handsome white tugs – their names were clear, *Hercules* and *Samson* – nosed up to their stations on either side of the ship and eased her up to her moorings in mid-harbour.

A sad young couple went down to breakfast and, when Andrew had finished, he went round the table saying goodbye to the others. He thanked the Allenbys particulary for being so friendly and helpful. He said to Lady Allenby, 'If things go the way I hope they will, and if someone I know will have me, you'll see a lot more of me!'

Lady Allenby got up and kissed him. 'I hope so, I really do hope so, Andy.'

Sarah left with Andy and went to his cabin with him to help with his last-minute packing, and to share some last intimate moments together. They were up on deck again just before ten when a very small white launch came alongside the pontoon which was moored to the ship. A young man in a white, open-necked shirt and white drill trousers came up the gangway at a run. He seemed to know his way about large liners because he started at once to make his way to the Purser's office. He was followed by a young Ceylonese man.

Andrew turned to Sarah. 'That's my man, I'm sure. This is not goodbye, my darling. I'm going to marry you one day, please never forget that and please, please, wait for me. I'm going to make this very short!' He kissed her and turned away hurriedly to follow the young man from the launch.

Before he crossed the transom, leading to the Purser's office, Andrew turned towards Sarah. 'There's a letter in your cabin, my darling.'

Andrew met the Agents' man outside the Purser's office. A purserette nodded towards Andrew as he approached, and the young man turned. 'Andrew Harvey?' he enquired.

'That's me,' said Andrew, holding out his hand.

The man shook it and said, 'My name is Martin Phillips, I'm from James Whittalls, your Colombo Agents, and this is Fernando, our wharf clerk. He will see your baggage into our launch which is waiting below. Are you ready to leave?'

'I am, and all my baggage is by the head of the gangway. I've said my goodbyes – I'm ready to go.'

'Come along, then. One of my Colombo friends is sailing on leave to Australia tonight and I'm coming back on board for a farewell drink. I shall look over this wonderful ship later on.' They moved to the gangway and went down to the Agents' launch. This was quite impressive, a gleaming white hull with polished mahogany panelling inside. The brass fittings fiercely reflected the morning sun. Two Sinhalese sailors held the launch snugly alongside the pontoon with boathooks. The coxswain remained at the wheel.

'We'll let your things come on board first,' said Phillips, looking up to the top of the gangway where Fernando was directing two of the ships' lascars towards Andrew's luggage. Andrew followed his gaze and saw Sarah at the rail looking down. Lady Allenby had an arm around her shoulders and they both waved. Andrew took off his new topee and waved it, then blew a kiss to Sarah.

Phillips ushered Andrew on board. 'A friend, perhaps?' he enquired.

'More than that, I hope,' said Andrew, 'but as I'm not allowed to marry on my first agreement we have a long separation ahead of us.' He moved to the stern of the launch and gave a final wave to Sarah and her mother.

'I know the feeling' said Martin Phillips, following him. 'I'm on my first agreement too, although I've only eight more months to wait before I get six months leave. On full pay!' he exclaimed.

Chapter 3

The journey to the passenger pier was short, and in ten minutes the launch had moored alongside the jetty. During the journey Phillips gave Andrew a brief resumé of the events that awaited him. 'You and I are going straight to the office to meet the directors. Fernando will take your luggage to my bungalow where you're going to spend the night. In the morning you'll be driven up to Strathmore which is the name of your tea estate. The directors will tell you all about your agreement with the Latimer Tea Company who own Strathmore and seven other tea estates. We don't call them "plantations" or "gardens" here – we call them "estates".'

The two young men passed through Customs, a pure formality, and walked to where Phillips had parked his car. The sun was now very hot and Andrew was surprised at the wave of humid air that hit him as he followed Martin Phillips. However, this heat was nothing compared to the temperature inside the locked car.

'Put your hand on the steering wheel,' said Martin. Andrew did, and pulled it away sharply. It felt red hot.

A short drive through The Fort and they parked outside the Agents' offices. 'The Fort' was the name for an area of about a square mile where the business centre of Colombo lay. All the main offices were located here, and so were some large shops, some British, but mostly Ceylonese or Indian. Jewellers and shops selling silk were in abundance. Andrew was impressed to see three or four British police sergeants mounted on fine horses patrolling The Fort area.

A uniformed peon opened Andrew's door and Martin came round to his side of the car. 'Don't be nervous,' he said. 'The directors are quite human and two of them, anyway, were planters themselves, some years ago, and so they will know how you are feeling this morning.'

Martin led the way to a lift and they went up to the top floor, the fifth, of the building. They went into a large office facing south, east and west through large glass windows. These were protected by shutters against the morning sun from the east and the afternoon sun from the west. The feature that took Andrew's eye at once was a number of punkhas slowly swinging to and fro across the room. These were being pulled by unseen 'punkha wallahs'.

Martin gave a nod to one or two young European men sitting at their desks and then moved over to the west end of the office where the directors' rooms were situated. He knocked and entered, with Andrew close behind him. A grey-haired man was sitting behind a large desk, but Andrew only gave him a glance; it was the view behind the figure that took all his attention. There were two very large plate-glass windows, and beyond these was an unbroken view of the sea. This was unbelievably blue, very calm, and a small fleet of fishing catamarans with rust-coloured sails stood off about half a mile from the shore. Being five storeys up the view seemed intensified.

The grey-haired figure behind the desk had risen to his feet and Andrew pulled himself together. However, there was no need for him to apologise for his seeming rudeness. The director was quite pleased, and he smiled and came forward with an outstretched hand. 'It's quite a view, isn't it? I sit with my back to it on purpose, otherwise I wouldn't get any work done. My name is Derek Scott and I know you are Andrew Harvey.' They shook hands. 'Come and sit down. Please stay, Martin. Draw up a chair. I shan't keep Harvey very long.'

The director opened a file in front of him. 'We heard about you from our London friends a week or two ago, and we have all the details of your new employment here,' the director said, tapping the file. He went on: 'We're glad you've decided on a tea planting career. It's a good life, a very pleasant life, and, provided you don't go to the club too many times a week, a very healthy life! I expect Martin has told you that your first posting is to be to Strathmore Estate. We call them "estates" in Ceylon; in India and elsewhere they're sometimes called "plantations" or "gardens". Yours is a tea estate in the Dimbula district of Ceylon. The average height of the estate is five thousand five hundred feet, and so you will have nice warm sunshine during daylight hours and pretty cold nights. The property is just under eight hundred acres in size, and it is planted entirely in tea. There is a large modern tea factory at just under five thousand feet and this copes quite easily with all the green leaf crop from the estate. There is a substantial and very attractive superintendent's bungalow and three smaller assistant superintendents' bungalows. You will be known as a "creeper" when you first start work and then, in a few months' time, when you know something about tea planting, you will carry the rank of assistant superintendent, in fact you will be referred to as an S.D., which is Tamil for *Sinna Dorai*, or 'little master'.'

The director continued: 'Your starting pay will be four hundred rupees a month, which is thirty pounds. This may not sound a lot but you must remember you get a free house, free electricity and firewood and a meat ration. Then you are given two indoor servants, a cook and a houseboy, and two gardeners. We shall make you a member of the Ceylon Planters Provident Fund and your employers, The Latimer Tea Company, have their own pension fund. The superintendent or manager, of Strathmore, is a Mr Sanders and he is called the P.D., or *Periya Dorai*. There are two assistant superintendents, and you will be living with one of these during your "creeping" days. Any questions?'

'No, sir, I don't think so. Not at the moment,' said Andrew.

'Good,' said the director, and added, 'One last thing. Martin here will take you round the shops now. They're only a few hundred yards away. You'll need some clothes for the estate and Martin will advise you. We shall settle the bill for what you buy. Now please don't feel offended; I had already noticed the topee you were carrying when you came into my office. You'll be laughed at if you wear that in Colombo or on the estate. It came from Simon Artz, didn't it?'

Andrew nodded.

'At least you didn't buy a red fez! But seriously, may I say we are glad to have you in our Agency and I know Mr Sanders will be very pleased to know you played cricket and rugger for your Oxford College. There is keen competition up-country between the various tea planting districts. I'm sure you'll be much in demand.'

The director got up and walked round his desk. 'Martin will explain how you will be driven up to Strathmore in the morning.' He held out his hand. 'Goodbye, Harvey, and good luck. Look in and see us whenever you're down in Colombo.'

As the two young men were leaving the office, Andrew asked, 'What shall I do with this?' He held out the offending topee.

Martin said, 'This is our head peon Sherriff, give it to him. He'll find a good home for it.' He took the helmet from Andrew and walked over to Sherriff. 'Here, Sherriff, this very fine topee, you wear it next time you go to your village, they will all think you are Governor General.'

Sherriff simpered and took the topee. He had a sense of humour too. 'Thank you very much, sir,' he said. 'I will give it to my Auntie to wear when she goes to church.'

'He likes to have his little joke,' said Martin. They walked from the office to Chatham Street passing the lighthouse on the corner, with its clock below the great light. They went into an Indian silk store called Lalchands. They were asked to sit down and fresh lime-juice drinks were produced. 'You are going to need khaki shorts and slacks and some short-sleeved shirts,' said Martin. 'I take it you have things like a suit and flannels and other clothes for the evenings?' Andrew said he had and, having selected the material, he was measured and then Martin took over. He started to tell the tailor about the cut and pattern of the shirts.

The tailor interrupted. 'Master going to be tea planter, no?'

Andrew nodded.

'Then Master no need to worry; I know exactly, Master will be wanting twelve shirts and six shorts. I have all ready by end of week and posting to Master on estate.'

After leaving Lalchands the two walked to York Street and into a large British store called Cargills. Here they bought Andrew a proper topee of the 'pig sticker' variety. Martin said, 'We'll walk back right round the square; it'll only take ten or fifteen minutes.'

At the first crossroads, Martin pointed ahead. 'That's the passenger jetty where you came ashore this morning.'

Andrew was interested in the number of Europeans he saw in rickshaws. 'What are these people doing?' he asked.

'They're brokers,' replied Martin. 'They go round all the offices and do their broking business. They're tea brokers, rubber brokers, freight brokers and so on. All the broking firms here have their own rickshaws and rickshaw pullers. The rickshaw pullers are incredible men. They drink a lot of toddy and arrack and smoke very strong Jaffna cheroots, yet they can run for half an hour non-stop. I don't think they live to a very great age!

'Now I'll drive you back to my bungalow,' said Martin when they returned to his car. 'Hop in.'

It took them about ten minutes to reach Martin's house which was down a lane, off the Galle Road, and leading to the sea. Andrew's luggage was already there, and a white-coated servant in a spotless white sarong greeted them. 'This is Suppiah, my boy,' said Martin, 'and he will look after you until I come back for lunch. You are being called for at ten o'clock tomorrow morning, so don't unpack everything. Just a clean shirt and a pair of slacks will do for this evening.'

Andrew hadn't been left alone for long when Martin Phillips telephoned. 'I've had an idea, Andrew,' he said. 'You remember that

I told you that I'm going back on board your ship this evening. Well, I can easily get a pass for you if you'd like to come on board too. It'll give you a chance to have a few more hours with your girlfriend and I'm sure she'd love it too.'

Andrew didn't take long to make up his mind. 'You're on, Martin,' he said. 'Thank you very much. I'd love to come back on board with you to see Sarah.' He unpacked a light tropical suit he had bought in London and waited impatiently for the evening and Martin's return from the office.

When Martin returned, they set off for the passenger jetty and found the office launch waiting for them. When they arrived at the liner, Andrew almost ran up the gangway and made his way to the Purser's office. The purserette who had dealt with him during the voyage recognised him at once. 'Shall I see if I can find Miss Allenby?'

Andrew was taken aback by the young officer's immediate reaction on recognising him.

'Yes please,' he stammered.

Sarah was located in her parents' drawing room. 'I have a call for you, Miss Allenby,' said the purserette. 'Please hold the line.' She passed the instrument over to Andrew.

'Hello, darling,' he said.

'Andy! What are you doing on board? Have you changed your mind? Are you travelling with us? Darling, please say you are.'

'No such luck,' said Andrew, 'but I'm on board until you sail. Can I see you?'

'You stay put, young man. I'll be with you in two shakes, as soon as I've told Mum and Dad you're on board.'

She was as good as her word and, as soon as the couple saw each other, they embraced fiercely, to the amusement of the purserette.

Sarah put her arm through Andrew's and led him away. 'This is marvellous, Andy. How have you managed to come aboard again?'

'Martin Phillips, who met me this morning, has a friend who is sailing with you tonight. He's going on six weeks leave to Australia where his parents live. He works in the Australian High Commission in Colombo. Anyway, when Martin said he could get me a pass to come on board again, I jumped at the chance. I do love you so, my darling. I don't know how I'm going to manage the next five years without you.'

'I feel the same,' said Sarah, 'but something will turn up, I'm sure. Thank you for that lovely letter you left me. I will treasure it. Dad is arranging for us to dine together, alone, and he's going to pay!'

After an intimate dinner together, the couple spent some time on the boat deck. Although a little humid, the night was fine and not too hot. The stars were brilliant and a full moon had just risen over the palm-fringed horizon to the east.

All too soon the 'All visitors and friends ashore, please' call came over the tannoy. They kissed once more and Andrew said, 'Stay here, darling. You can see our launch by the pontoon. Stay here, and I'll wave to you from below. In fact he waved more than once and gave a final wave as the launch passed under the stern of a Bibby liner anchored close by.

Andrew was awakened the next morning by Martin's bearer bringing him his early-morning tea. Andrew then had a cold shower and dressed in the same cotton suit he had bought in London and which he had worn when seeing Sarah the night before. At half past eight they left for Martin's office where a large Buick saloon was waiting. The Tamil driver, and a peon from Martin's office, transferred Andrew's luggage to the Buick.

'This is the Superintendent's car from Strathmore, Andrew,' said Martin. 'The driver's name is Muttusamy and he will drive you up to the estate.' Muttusamy salaamed and handed Andrew a letter which he opened then and there. It was from Peter Sanders, the Superintendent, welcoming him to Strathmore.

Andrew shook hands with Martin and thanked him for looking after him so well during his first few hours in Colombo. He then settled himself in the front seat of the Buick next to Muttusamy and they started their journey.

Muttusamy's English was pretty good. He asked Andrew if this was his first visit to Ceylon. Andrew said it was, and so the driver went briefly over the route he was going to take. 'First, sir, we drive through The Fort, then we go past the harbour to the Pettah. The Pettah is a lot of Indian silk shops, and then we go over the Kelani river and on to the Kandy road. In a little more than two hours we arrive in Kandy. Master will have lunch at the Queens Hotel and after that I will drive him to the estate.'

'What about your lunch, Muttusamy?' asked Andrew.

'Sanders *dorai* has given me batta. This means money for my rice. I will go to a small hotel and there I will have rice and curry. The curry we eat is very hot, very tasty, with lots of chillies. Master will be having many curries on Sundays but not so hot as our curries.'

They drove over the large and very impressive steel bridge that spanned the Kelani river. They then forked right on to the Kandy road and Andrew settled himself comfortably to take in the strange but colourful villages they were beginning to pass through. First he took off his jacket and tossed it onto the back seat because the temperature in the car was rising steadily, despite the fact that Muttusamy had the windows open.

They had been driving for about half an hour when they saw a horseman approaching. As they drew closer, Muttusamy slowed down, and Andrew could see that the horse was a very solid cob, its short legs immense. Astride was an elderly Sinhalese gentleman beautifully dressed in a tussore silk jacket and waistcoat and white drill jodhpurs. He wore a khaki topee and carried a riding crop.

Muttusamy slowed down to a crawl. 'Wave, master,' said Muttusamy hurriedly. Andrew did and the figure, in a most dignified way, raised his topee and crop.

'You know who that is, sir?' asked Muttusamy, accelerating.

'No, I don't,' said Andrew.

'He is Sir Solomon Dias Bandaranaike – a very fine, famous gentleman, a real gentleman. He owns a lot of property in this place.'

A little while later Muttusamy turned to Andrew. 'Soon, sir, we coming to very bad spot. Here there are many naughty ladies, up to no good, sir. They very tricksy.'

'What do you mean, Muttusamy, what is "tricksy"?' asked Andrew.

'Don't you know, sir? They stopping lorry drivers and taking them into their huts for you know what, sir!'

Andrew had a fair idea of what Muttusamy meant but he wanted to learn more.

'Tell me about these naughty ladies, Muttusamy. What do they do to lorry drivers?'

'Well, sir,' said Muttusamy, 'in two or three miles we will see many many small tables with big lots of cashew nuts on them. Behind every table is a young woman who is selling her cashew nuts. She is also selling something else, sir. She is selling her, you know what, to passing lorry drivers who want some jiggery-pokery. Very naughty ladies, master.'

'Have *you* ever stopped here, Muttusamy?' asked Andrew.

'Sometimes I am thinking about stopping here, sir, but then I think if Mrs Muttusamy ever finds out she will kill me, so I drive on pretty dam' quick.'

'Well, you go past these ladies "pretty dam' slow", Muttusamy. I want to have a good look,' said Andrew, and he thought that perhaps a planter's life was not going to be so bad after all.

Muttusamy giggled and said, 'Here they are, master.'

Along the left side of the road there were twenty or thirty small wooden tables with cashew nuts in large heaps on each, just as Muttusamy had said. Behind each little table was a young woman aged in her early twenties. They were dressed pretty much alike. Each wore a colourful sarong which stopped below her navel. Then each girl wore a skintight, very short, white bodice leaving a six inch gap of deliciously brown skin adorned by her navel. Their raven black hair was swept back and a frangipane flower added a white and yellow splash of colour behind one ear. Their red lips and perfect white teeth gave Andrew all the evidence he needed to confirm that Muttusamy's belief, that they had more than just cashew nuts on offer, was quite correct.

Some of the 'naughty ladies' gave Andrew a wave – they all gave him a smile – and Muttusamy drove on.

'That must be a very large horse,' said Andrew pointing to a large heap of dung in the middle of the road.

'Not horse, sir, elephant,' said Muttusamy. 'Looks very fresh, perhaps we may see elephant.' He was quite right. A mile further on there was an enormous tusker ahead of them. He was carrying his supper coiled up in his trunk. His supper consisted of a large sheaf of banana leaves and a small section of the trunk of the tree. Muttusamy overtook the elephant and stopped the car. They got out and awaited the arrival of the tusker and his mahout. When they were a few yards away the mahout stopped his elephant and gave it a command. The beast raised its off foreleg and the mahout stepped onto the bent knee and jumped to the ground.

Muttusamy spoke to the man in Sinhalese and then turned to Andrew. 'The elephant driver says that they have been moving logs in a rubber estate since early morning and now the elephant is going home to have a rest and at four o'clock he will be allowed to eat his supper. The mahout says that he would like to make the elephant give you a *salaam* but if he did he would drop his food and it would take some time to pick it all up again. Perhaps master would like to give him a small present?'

'How much do you think I should give?' asked Andrew.

'One rupee, that will be enough to buy him his rice and curry for tonight and also a glass of toddy or arrack.'

'What is arrack?' asked Andrew, having heard the word before but never asking what it meant.

41

'Toddy comes from the coconut tree, from the milk in the coconut, it is white and tastes smoky. Arrack I am not sure about, but I think they do something to the toddy to make it look like whisky but not so brown. Arrack is very strong and makes you feel like having high jinks.'

They passed through a town on a hill called Kegalle and climbed towards the little town of Mawanella a few miles on and stopped on the bridge.

'Come out of the car, master, come near these big trees,' said Muttusamy, 'but do not make a noise.' They crossed to the side wall of the bridge and Muttusamy clapped his hands and shouted. Andrew couldn't believe his eyes or his ears. Hundreds of flying foxes dropped from their upside-down sleep and took to the air screaming with fright. He had never before seen such a sight and the giant bats showed no inclination to return to their slumbers but kept on wheeling in the air and calling stridently.

Andrew was just about to return to the car when Muttusamy called urgently to him. 'Master, master, come here quickly, look.'

Andrew saw what he thought was a baby crocodile crawling across the road. 'Is that a crocodile, Muttusamy?' he asked.

'No, sir, not crocodile, that we call "Kabragoya", it is like giant lizard. It will not bite you, they are very frightened creatures and they will run away. Must keep away from their tail. One hit from Kabragoya's tail and you have broken legs.'

Andrew watched fascinated as the five- or six-foot-long creature slowly crossed the road, its black tongue flicking in and out.

Back in the car they approached the Kadugannawa Pass, the pass that leads into Kandy through the hill some seventeen hundred feet above Colombo. In the middle of the Pass they went through a spectacular rock tunnel. This appeared to be a gigantic boulder that had fallen, many, many years ago, from the hillside above, onto the road below, and the engineers had tunnelled through the solid rock.

Up they went, travelling through the poinsettia hedges, with their scarlet flowers, that lined the road to Peradeniya, and on through the Kandy market to the Queens Hotel.

Muttusamy pointed out the Kandy Lake in front of the hotel and the Dalada Maligawa, more commonly known as the Temple of the Tooth. Although a Tamil, and a Hindu himself, Muttusamy proudly explained the reason for the name. He said, 'Very long time ago, sir, it is said, that the Lord Buddha was here and that in this temple his sacred tooth is enshrined. Once a year the tooth is taken in a big procession of elephants round Kandy so that all the people can see and worship. They call this the "Pera Hera". It is very fine sight, sir. Many elephants, all decorated, and tom-toms, and lights and crackers. Master must come down from estate and see.'

Muttusamy parked the Buick and took himself off to have his lunch. Andrew made his way into the cool interior of the hotel and washed his hands in the gentlemen's toilets before making his way to the bar and ordering a beer.

The bartender said, 'This beer made here, sir, in Nuwara Eliya, up the hill there.' He pointed. 'I am telling master this because I think from his fine suit he is new to Ceylon.'

Andrew sipped his beer and took it with him to the palm-fringed dining room where the electric fans were turning overhead. He had a good lunch, fried seer fish and roast chicken, followed by some fresh mango fool.

After lunch he made his way to the car, feeling just a little apprehensive as to what might be waiting for him at the end of the journey. The feeling reminded him of the first day at a new school. However, he need not have worried.

Muttusamy was waiting in the Buick, and they started their two-hour climb up the Ramboda Pass to their destination, Strathmore Estate. The journey was uneventful, except for the fact that Andrew felt a little carsick. This was not surprising because, in the three to four thousand feet climb to Strathmore from Kandy, there was scarcely a hundred yard stretch of straight road without a sharp corner or a hairpin bend.

The views were breathtaking and, to Andrew, there seemed to be tea bushes everywhere. Every hillside was a sheet of green, and Andrew wondered how the tea pluckers could move between the bushes to do their work. There were some lakes and waterfalls to be admired as they drove up the pass and the villagers' clothing got heavier as they climbed to over four thousand feet, a chill starting to set in.

Chapter 4

At last Muttusamy turned off the main road on to the estate cart road and, after a mile or so, turned left at a fork signposted 'Superintendent's Bungalow'. Andrew felt his stomach tighten, and he tried to quell the nervousness he was feeling. He felt better when the house came into view, and his nervousness gave way to admiration. The house was of white stone and he saw it was a single-storeyed bungalow. It had a green corrugated iron roof and was surrounded by the most magnificent trees. There were grevilleas, albizzias and some beautiful tulip trees with their dark green leaves and scarlet flowers. When the garden came into full view, Andrew was astonished at the enormous green lawns, all immaculate, and bordered with flowers of every description, including roses which surprised him. He had no idea that roses could grow in a tropical country – but then, he had forgotten he was now at five thousand feet.

The drive up to the house was lined with begonias and he noticed that garden coolies were at work.

As the Buick drove under the porch, a servant in a white sarong and white buttoned-up tunic arrived on the spacious verandah. Muttusamy came round the car to open Andrew's door but he was already out and making his way towards the verandah. Two golden retrievers came bounding out to greet him with furiously wagging tails. They were competing with each other to put their paws on Andrew's chest when a pleasant voice called out, 'Down, Stock, down Trigger; this is no way in which to welcome Mr Harvey!'

An attractive woman with greying hair came forward and put out her hand. 'I'm so sorry about that, but these dogs are over-friendly; they simply love visitors.' She went on: 'I'm Angela Sanders; my husband is out on the estate somewhere, but I expect him back for tea in a little while.' She turned towards the car. 'Muttusamy, leave Harvey *dorai*'s saman in the car – you will be driving him down to one of the S.D.'s bungalows after tea.'

'Very good, lady,' replied Muttusamy.

'Come and sit down, Mr. Harvey, but perhaps you would like to freshen up first?' said Angela Sanders.

'Thank you very much, I would,' said Andrew, and went on: 'I don't know what the form is here but, if it is allowed, please call me Andrew, if you would like to.'

'Yes, I would like to, Andrew. We call our other S.D.s by their Christian names. You put that very nicely, if I may say so. I'll show you where our cloakroom is.' She went inside the bungalow, leading the way.

Having shown him the cloakroom, she said, 'I'll be outside on the verandah. Please come and join me when you are ready.'

When Andrew returned to the verandah, he found Mrs Sanders reading the morning paper which had just arrived in the estate's post bag, or tappal bag, as it was known here.

'This is the morning paper, Andrew,' she said. 'The train from Colombo brings us our post and papers every day, and a tappal coolie collects everything from the village and brings it up here.'

Mrs Sanders and Andrew chatted away, and a little while later they heard the clatter of horses' hooves. 'Here's my husband,' said Mrs Sanders and Andrew saw a fine chestnut horse turn the last bend towards the bungalow. Astride was a tall, thin man in an open-necked checked shirt and khaki slacks. He wore a double terai – a wide-brimmed, double thickness, felt hat – on his head. A horse-keeper, or syce, appeared from one end of the porch and went to the horse's head. After the superintendent dismounted the syce led the chestnut away.

Peter Sanders gave his hat and his switch to the bearer who had met Andrew and walked up the steps to the verandah. He was tall – not as tall as Andrew's six foot three, but nevertheless, over six feet. Andrew was impressed by his sunburnt face and arms. These were really tanned and the superintendent looked the picture of health.

He held out his hand. 'And how is my new creeper? You must be Andrew Harvey.'

The men shook hands and Sanders said, 'I'll just have a quick wash and I'll be back in a minute or two.' The second servant brought in a large silver tray and the head-boy followed with sandwiches and a cake.

Peter Sanders reappeared a few minutes later and they moved to a side verandah which led to the drawing room. They sat on cane chairs upholstered in colourful chintz.

The verandah faced west and the view over the garden towards the tea-covered hills was superb. For the first time Andrew was conscious of a slight drop in temperature and he recalled the Colombo Agent's remark about warm days and cold nights.

'Well, welcome to Strathmore, Harvey. Did Muttusamy look after you on the way up?'

'He was marvellous, sir. He was a fount of information and the Buick is a lovely car.'

Angela Sanders interrupted. 'Andrew would like us to call him "Andrew",' she said.

'Good,' said Peter Sanders, and went on: 'I called you a "creeper" just now, and that is how you will be known for a month or two until you know a little about tea planting. When that happens I will promote you as one of my S.D.s or *sinna dorais*. We have two S.D.s at present but, as the senior one is being transferred to another estate belonging to our Company, you are going to fill the vacancy. My junior S.D. has a nice bungalow and you will live and mess with him – his name is Alan Ferguson – until the senior one moves on and then you will have Alan's bungalow to yourself and he will move to the vacant bungalow.' He smiled. 'Not too complicated, I hope.'

'Not at all, sir,' said Andrew.

'I'm so glad you play cricket and rugger,' said Sanders. 'We're all pretty sport minded up here and we play against the other districts and, in August, we go down to Colombo and play against them. Which game do you prefer?'

'I like both, sir. I played cricket and rugger for my college at Oxford, but I wasn't good enough for a Blue. I like tennis, too.'

'Good,' said the Superintendent. 'Now a few points about your work. Whilst you're a creeper and an S.D. you will have a pretty early morning start, around six o'clock. You will attend muster – that is what we call it. It means that you will be present to see that all the coolies have reported for work. There are a lot of them, over a thousand in fact. We have nearly eight hundred acres here on Strathmore, all planted in tea, and it is general practice to have about a coolie and a half for each acre.'

'What do they all do, sir?' asked Andrew.

'Well, the women coolies do the plucking and the men have plenty to do weeding, pruning, manuring and so on. Then there are some more people in the factory. Apart from the coolies, there are the more senior staff. There are Kanganies – they are sort of foremen – then there is the Teamaker, and we have a doctor and a dispenser in our little hospital, together with some nursing staff. There is a schoolmaster and all sorts of other people. Don't worry too much about all this; you'll find you'll soon get to know the ropes.' He went on: 'The junior S.D. with whom you are going to live for the time being is, as I've said, Alan Ferguson. You'll like him, I'm sure. He's a little older than you and we're very pleased with his work. I will arrange for Ferguson to bring you to the factory at, say, nine o'clock in the morning and I'll show you all the machinery and explain how we turn the green leaf we pluck from the bushes into black tea. In the afternoon I'll drive you round the whole property so that you know the rough layout. Ask all the questions you like, and I'll answer them. Oh, and one more thing: you'll have to start learning Tamil. This can easily be arranged, but it is vital that you learn the language. For one thing, the workforce – that is to say, the coolies – will respect you all the more if you can talk to them and joke with them in their own language. They love to be teased and joked with. Our schoolmaster will teach you Tamil and you can make your own appointments with him to come to your bungalow. Tamil is quite fun, actually, especially when you translate English phrases or remarks into Tamil. For example, the Tamil word for "go" is "po" and the Tamil word for "good" is "nulla" so, what a lot of us say, when leaving a party, is, "We'd better po whilst the po-ing is nulla!"'

'And now,' Peter Sanders went on, 'I'll drive you down to Alan Ferguson's bungalow.'

Andrew rose to his feet and, thanking Mrs Sanders for his tea, followed the P.D. to the car. 'You can go, Muttusamy' said Sanders. 'I'll drive Harvey *dorai* to the small S.D.'s bungalow.'

After a few minutes' drive down some sandy and gravelly roads, they turned off along a short tarmac drive to Alan Ferguson's bungalow. This, too, was charming. Although smaller than the P.D.'s bungalow, the colours were the same: white walls and a green roof, and the house was set in a very pretty and immaculate garden.

Swinging a golf club on the lawn was the S.D. He dropped the club and walked over to the car and opened the driver's door. 'Good evening, sir,' he said.

'Hello, Alan. This is our new creeper, Andrew Harvey,' said the P.D.

Ferguson came round the car as Andrew was getting out. They shook hands as Peter Sanders watched approvingly, leaning on the bonnet of the car. They made a good-looking couple of young men. He noted that Alan Ferguson was not quite as tall as Andrew's six foot three, but he was over six feet and perhaps a little broader. He was blond, and his face, arms and knees were very brown.

'Where's your saman – sorry, your baggage?' asked Alan. They both moved round to the boot of the Buick to get it out.

'Well, I'll leave you two to settle in,' said the P.D. and, before he drove off, he turned to Alan and said, 'Please bring Andrew to the factory at nine tomorrow morning, Alan. I intend to spend most of tomorrow with him showing him round and explaining what tea planting and tea manufacturing is all about.'

'We'll be there, sir,' said Alan.

Between them they carried Andrew's suitcase and a couple of small bags to the porch of the bungalow. A servant in a white open-necked shirt and a white sarong came hurrying out of the house. He salaamed Andrew.

'This is Sellamuttu, my head boy,' said Alan. 'He'll take your things to your room and unpack for you if you like. Is this all you've got?'

'No, I'm having some shorts and shirts and one or two other things made in Colombo, and they are posting them up to me in a few days' time.'

'They are all Indian tailors, you know,' said Alan, 'and their work is very, very good. They're best at copying, but they make things to measure as well, and you won't believe the speed at which they can make and deliver clothes. Did you know that they come on board a liner when it docks early in the morning in Colombo, measure passengers and deliver suits and shirts and anything else they order before the ship sails at night. It's quite marvellous.'

They walked into the house, which was a three-bedroomed affair. It was bright and cheerful, and the broad verandahs that surrounded three quarters of the bungalow let in a pleasant draught of fresh, but chilly, air. There was a large drawing room and a good-sized dining room. The garden was colourful and immaculate.

'Do you do all the gardening yourself?' asked Andrew.

'Good heavens, no,' said Alan. 'The Company gives me two gardeners – garden coolies we call them – and they do all the work under my supervision. I also get a free cook and then there's a low caste Tamil coolie who deals with the lavatories. When I go to the other S.D.'s bungalow they will all stay here with you except Sellamuttu. I employ him myself and he'll come with me wherever I go. I'll get Sellamuttu to find someone for you to look at. You should have a good look at him and be sure you like him. He will be your personal servant and he will look after your clothes and shoes, draw your bath and generally take care of you.'

He turned to Andrew. 'Forgive me asking, but do you like girls? I mean, do you have girl friends? I ask for a special reason.'

'Yes, I do like the opposite sex! Very much so. In fact I've just said a very sad farewell to a girl on the ship. I hope to marry her when this first agreement of mine is over in five years' time. Why do you ask?'

'I ask because the senior S.D., who has just been transferred to another estate, and who is living in the other S.D.'s bungalow at present, is not fond of girls. He prefers boys, the younger the better. It was awful. He made a pass or two at me in the early days. When he found out that there was nothing doing, he used to arrange with his servant to bring up a small boy from the lines once a week or so. Thank goodness he's going.'

Andrew digested this startling news and changed the subject. 'What are "the lines"?' he asked.

'It's where the coolies live with their wives and families. You'll see them tomorrow when the P.D. takes you round the estate. Visitors from abroad, who usually know nothing about these things, think we house our coolies in abominable conditions. Some do sleep six or eight to a room I admit, but if our visitors saw the conditions in which these people live in their own villages in India, they wouldn't be so critical.'

Alan went on: 'It'll be only you and me for dinner this evening, I'm afraid. Depending on what I'm doing, I usually call for my first drink about half past six and then Sellamuttu runs my bath. I only wear slacks, an open-necked shirt and a sweater for dinner and – oh, you must get yourself a pair of mosquito boots. They're marvellous for the evenings when one is not dressed up. They're made of very soft elk hide and they go inside your slacks and stop just below the knee. I'll run you up to Nuwara Eliya one weekend if you like and we'll order a pair for you. Mosquitos are troublesome here at night, that's why there's a net over your bed.'

'You said "elk" hide just now,' said Andrew. 'What sort of elk do you have here?'

'In fact they're large Indian deer,' said Alan, 'of the Sambhur family – there are a lot of them about in our jungles and on some of our up-country plains. Their skins are wonderfully soft and supple and make fine boots and other leather goods.'

'Yes, we'll go to Nuwara Eliya one weekend soon,' continued Alan. 'We'll do some shopping and then have lunch at the Grand Hotel where we can spend the night. On my next agreement, depending on where I'm posted, I'd like to join the Hill Club in Nuwara Eliya. It's

49

awfully good and I've had one or two riotous sessions in a small bar there called "The Snake Pit". The Hill Club is remarkable in some ways. It seems to hang on to many of the traditions of one's father's days. I mean, there's silver – real silver – on the tables at meal-times, the servants wear white gloves, there's an open fire burning away in one's room when it's time to retire. One's bath is prepared when it is required, and so on. It's all very luxurious, and then, of course, there's the golf club opposite with a full supplement of leeches waiting for you.'

'I thought leeches were for medical use in the old days,' said Andrew.

'That's true, but these go for the golfer in dozens at some holes!'

'A bit off-putting, surely?'

'You will get used to them, but they *are* revolting, and the girls hate them, of course. I'll show you some one Sunday. Now we'd better have our baths. We'll take a drink in with us.'

Sellamuttu came into Andrew's room early the next morning and started pulling up his mosquito net. 'Early-morning tea, sir,' he said.

The two young men sat down to a good breakfast at eight o'clock and then made their way to Alan's car. Andrew had done quite a lot of sunbathing with Sarah on the ship, and so his arms and knees were fairly brown. They were certainly not the deathly white that some young men, newly out from England, had to show. He felt strange in shorts they were quite unlike Alan's 'Ceylon' shorts – and he looked forward to receiving his parcel of clothes from the tailor in Colombo.

They drove up to the factory passing tea pluckers at work. Some of these women were quite attractive and Andrew was amused to see the shy, but admiring, glances they gave Alan from partly lowered eyes. Some of the bolder ones stared at Andrew too and no doubt wondered who this good-looking newcomer was.

The factory was a vast silver-coloured building. It consisted of four storeys and was constructed of corrugated-iron sheets painted a light shade of aluminium. At first sight, the upper storeys seemed to consist of nothing but windows, and Andrew wondered why. There was a muffled roar coming from the building and, here again, Andrew wondered where the noise was coming from.

Alan stopped the car and they got out and walked to one end of the factory. They climbed three steps and found themselves on a large cement-floored verandah. Pluckers were already bringing in their baskets full of green leaf which they emptied onto tables on the verandah floor. Factory supervisors, or Kanganies, examined the leaf and, if they were satisfied that only 'two leaves and a bud' had been plucked, that plucker's name was marked down for payment. A wonderful smell of green tea swept over Andrew and he longed to ask questions.

However, there was no time for questions, because a few minutes later the Superintendent arrived. 'Good morning, gentlemen,' said Peter Sanders and, turning to Alan, enquired, 'What are you doing this morning, Alan?'

'Two things, sir,' said Alan. 'Firstly, I'm going to look at the weeders working in Upper Division and secondly, I would like to go to the nurseries to see how our vegetative propagation is getting on. I'm very optimistic about those new clones we're trying out. I've got a feeling that they're going to improve our yield per acre enormously.'

'I hope you're right,' said the P.D. 'Well, off you go and I'll drop Andrew back at your bungalow at lunch time.' Then, addressing Andrew, he said, 'Now, Andrew, come with me and ask as many questions as you like.' They turned towards the piles of green leaf.

'The pluckers – they're all women – start very early in the mornings and they bring in their baskets as soon as they're full,' said Sanders. 'The Kanganies examine the green leaf very carefully, because the whole quality of the tea we produce depends on the fineness of the leaf that is plucked. You see, Andrew, the pluckers are paid by weight for the tea they bring in from the field, so they sometimes try and get away with coarse plucking, that is to say they pluck below the "two leaves and a bud" regulation. They take, say, three leaves and a bud and this gives them more weight for less plucking. The snag is that if the pluckers "pluck coarse" you get stalk in your tea, what people call a "stranger" in your tea cup.' Peter Sanders took Andrew by the shoulder. 'Look over there,' he said. 'That woman has been found out!' Andrew looked towards a small group where a lot of angry squabbling was going on. 'The Kangani has found some coarse leaf in her basket and she'll get no pay.'

They moved up a wooden staircase and Andrew saw rows and rows of wooden racks with jute hessian spread across them. Green leaf had been spread along the hessian and some enormous fans were making the roar that Andrew heard when he and Alan were driving up to the factory.

Peter Sanders explained. 'This is a withering loft, it's where we wither, or dry the tea.' He went on. 'When the green leaf is plucked, Andrew, it still has a lot of moisture in it and these great fans extract the moisture and make the leaf dry. We have three lofts like this, two more above this one. One snag is that the fans also remove the moisture from the pine board linings of the walls of the lofts, the floorboards and everything else. This makes the whole factory into a veritable tinder box and the risk of fire is enormous. The insurance companies don't like insuring tea factories, as you can imagine, and the premiums are very high.'

'But there's no fire up here, sir,' said Andrew. 'Everything is beautifully fresh and cool and I can't think how a fire could start.'

'Wait and see,' said Sanders. 'When we go downstairs to the drier room you'll see there's a lot of fire and heat down there. Also, of course, there's the risk of malicious damage. I speak from experience. When I was your age I was creeping on another estate in the Bogowantalawa district. The engine driver, the man who looks after the big Ruston Hornsby engines we use to drive our machinery, discovered that the Teamaker was having an affair with his wife. So, to get his revenge, the silly clot set fire to the factory. One match in one of these lofts was quite enough, and in an hour or so the whole factory was destroyed. What the silly man intended to do was to put the Teamaker out of a job. The idiot didn't realise that he would put himself out of a job as well! Plus, of course, a lot of other factory workers.'

'Anyway,' the Superintendent continued, 'a lot of tea companies, ours included, are having their factories equipped with a sprinkler system. These are marvellous things and every ten square feet or so the ceilings have a sprinkler head. At the first sign of an increase in temperature the sprinkler head explodes and a strong jet of water puts the fire out. Someone told me once that the force of the water is so great that a man could not stand under it – it would knock him over. I think this is an exaggeration probably put about by the sprinkler manufacturers. Anyway, a sprinkler system cuts the fire insurance premium by nearly a half. Anyway, to continue: Once the green leaf is withered,' said Sanders, 'it's taken down to the rollers downstairs. Come with me.'

The two men went down the wooden staircase. The Superintendent pointed to some large green machines. 'These are the rollers, Andrew,' he said. 'The withered leaf is brought down from the lofts and fed into these rollers. The object of the exercise is to roll or squeeze the leaf so that all the valuable juices inside are released and cover the inside and outside of the leaf.'

The scent of green tea was now very strong. 'Once the withered leaf is rolled, for the first time, it is then spread out so that a period of fermentation can take place. I wont confuse you with the time each process takes, you'll find out all the details as you pay more and more visits to the factory. From here we go to the driers. The most popular make is the "Sirocco", so called after a hot dry wind from north Africa which blows over southern Italy. The rolled and fermented leaf is fed into these driers and the furnaces turn the green, withered and rolled leaf into black tea. Now this tea is all shapes and sizes, and so it has to be sorted into the regulation sizes of OP, BOP, BOPF, etc. etc. The letters stand for Orange Pekoe, Broken Orange Pekoe, Broken Orange Pekoe Fannings and so on. There's a final, very small grade which we call "Dust".'

The Superintendent and the Creeper moved into the sifting room. 'This is how we sort out our grades,' said Sanders. 'These sifters have trays of various grades of mesh, as you see, and the top tray retains the big Orange Pekoe leaf and the smaller grades work their way through to the bottom where the Dust collects.'

The Superintendent went on: 'Finally, the finished tea is looked over for stalk and any other undesirable foreign bodies before it is packed in these plywood chests ready for sale in Colombo, or shipment. All clear so far, Andrew?'

'Yes, I think so, sir, but, if you agree, I'd like to spend quite a lot of my time initially in the factory until I really understand tea manufacture,' said Andrew.

'Yes, of course,' said the Superintendent. 'A good idea. Alan and I will arrange your days so that you spend equal time outside, "in the field", as we say, and in the factory. Now I'll run you over to Alan and we'll see how he's getting on this morning. After that I'll take you round some of the estate and, once again, please ask as many questions as you like.'

They found Alan in the nurseries and he seemed quite excited. 'I think some of these new clones are going to give us nearly two thousand pounds an acre, sir,' he said, and went on: 'I've never seen such growth, and I'm sure the T.R.I. will be excited and surprised when they look at our nurseries. I don't think we should tell them, though, until we are sure of the yield.'

'The T.R.I. is The Tea Research Institute,' explained Peter Sanders, 'and they give us valuable advice on the hundred and one problems that confront us from time to time.'

They returned to the car and the Superintendent drove Andrew round the estate, stopping to visit the crèche and the small hospital and, finally, the school room. Andrew was very impressed by all he saw, and found many questions to ask. This pleased Peter Sanders.

Later, as the Creeper and the Superintendent were descending from one of the top divisions of the estate with a very steep drop on Andrew's side of the car, Andrew was puzzled to see that, instead of green luxuriant tea, there were acres of bare brown stumps sticking out of the precipitous hillside below him. These had spikes with terrifyingly sharp ends pointing upwards. 'What are those, sir?' he asked.

'They're pruned tea bushes, Andrew. At regular intervals the older tea is pruned to encourage growth. It looks awful now, but you watch it every time you visit this division. You'll be surprised at the speed with which the new green shoots appear. Not only does it look awful now, but this hillside can be dangerous too.'

'What do you mean?' asked Andrew, puzzled.

Peter Sanders laughed. 'Quite often our coolies come back from the town, having drunk too much toddy. This is usually late at night and sometimes they stagger off this cart road and fall over into the pruned tea. On occasions I've seen men almost literally crucified on the pruned tea and our poor doctor has much stitching up to do. It's funny in one sense, but really it can be very life-threatening!'

The afternoon went quickly enough, and soon it was teatime and the Superintendent dropped Andrew back at Alan's bungalow. He saw some letters on the hall table and was delighted to see that two were addressed to him.

Sellamuttu appeared. 'These letters were brought just now by the tappal coolie, sir.'

Andrew saw at once that one letter was from his father and the other from Sarah. Naturally, he opened Sarah's first. It was so affectionate that he read and re-read it before he turned to his father's letter. Whilst Sarah's letter had made him feel sad in the sense that he was desperate to see her again, and he knew this would not be for a long, long time, his father's letter cheered him up enormously. He had written to say that his missing accountant had been found and, to the great surprise of the police and everyone else, he had not disposed of any of the fortunes he had stolen. Mr Harvey wrote:

'I can't tell you how relieved your mother and I are at this surprising turn of events. We always knew the old scoundrel would be caught but we never imagined for a moment that he would have left my fortune, and some other people's fortunes too, more or less intact.

So, to show you how relieved I am, I'm enclosing a cheque for two thousand pounds with your mother's and my love. Your bank in Colombo will know how to clear this and they will credit your account with Ceylon rupees – just over twenty-six thousand, I think.

That is not all. I propose to give you an allowance of two thousand pounds a year because I know your creeper's salary is not very much. I hope this will make you feel independent. Having a small private income always helps one. You can perhaps buy a small car now.'

Andrew was over the moon. When Alan arrived back a little later, Andrew was looking round the garden. 'Alan, you said you would take me up to Nuwara Eliya one weekend. Are you still going to do this?'

'Of course,' said Alan. 'I'm sure you'll enjoy the little outing. You've got some new ideas as to what you want to do, haven't you?'

'You're very quick on the uptake!' said Andrew. 'Yes, I certainly have. I've just had a letter from my father who has had some good news. He has sent me a cheque and so I would like to look at some cars in Nuwara Eliya. I suppose there are car showrooms in the town?'

'Yes, not as many as there are in Colombo, but there's a Ford dealer and another place that keeps Morris Minors and other cars. You'll certainly be able to pick up something you'd like.'

As the two were talking, a rather old and decrepit motorcycle came slowly up Alan's short drive. Astride it was a middle-aged man wearing a rather crumpled white drill suit. 'This is old Murugiah, our school master,' said Alan. 'I expect he's come to see you about your Tamil lessons. He's a very nice man and he'll have you talking like a coolie in no time at all!'

Murugiah and Andrew took their seats on a stone bench under a tree in the garden, and it was agreed that Andrew would have two lessons a week. Murugiah jokingly warned him that he would have a lot of homework to do.

Andrew then turned his attention once again to Sarah's letter. He realised just how much he missed her, and he knew from this that he was seriously in love. He went to his room and wrote a long reply.

Chapter 5

A few weeks later Alan told Peter Sanders that he and Andrew would like to go to Nuwara Eliya for the weekend, and when he mentioned to the Superintendent that Andrew wanted to buy a car the P.D. was very pleased. This was because he had been wondering what Andrew was going to do for transport. He had thought he might ask Andrew if he could ride a horse.

The two young men left the estate early on the Saturday morning for Nuwara Eliya. Just before they climbed the final hill into the town, Alan stopped the car at a signpost on the right saying 'Mahagastotte Estate'.

'This is an interesting tea estate,' said Alan. 'It belongs to the Nuwara Eliya Tea Estate Company, and they have five or six very valuable properties in these hills. They produce wonderful high grown teas which usually command a premium in the Colombo auctions. More sportingly though, The Ceylon Motor Sports Club members are allowed to have their Easter hill climb every year on a hilly stretch of road on Mahagastotte. The road is very steep, very winding and it's surfaced with loose gravel which makes hill climbing at speed quite exciting, to say the least. The worst corners, over five or six thousand feet high, are sandbagged, but even then people go over the side. One particular Colombo wallah seems to make a habit of this, and rumour has it that he's never in his life seen the finish line.

Historically, though, Mahagastotte has a division called "Bakers Farm" and this is because Sir Samuel Baker, the great explorer, made his first camp here in the last century. Gentlemen of means in those days travelled with their Brewer in their entourage. One day, soon after he had settled down, Sir Samuel said to his Brewer, "Well – get brewing!" or words to that effect. So the Brewer went off exploring for a source of good, clean water, which is the first essential in making beer. He had to go a few miles but, in the end, he found a wonderful stream and a cascade at nearly seven thousand feet. This was called Hospital Falls and a small waterfall descended from the stream. Well,

Sir Samuel's brewer set up his still at the foot of the fall, and this morning I'll show you the huge Ceylon Brewery that has developed from that modest little still. But first let's look for your motorcar; after we've had a beer, of course!'

They sat on the lawn in glorious, but cool, sunshine in front of the Grand Hotel. A waiter in a white coat, buttoned up to the neck, and wearing a white sarong appeared at Alan's elbow. Alan said, 'Andrew, I'm not going to ask you what you would like because you must have some of the Nuwara Eliya beer I was telling you about. I rather like to plug these beers because I play golf with one of the assistant brewers and we're great friends. I'll get him to take us over the brewery one day; you'll love it.' He gave the order to the waiter.

Two tankards of beer arrived and Andrew had to admit it was very, very good. It was strong, too, because, by the time they went to the car to find a motor dealer, he felt very happy indeed.

He turned to Alan. 'And you say that this all started with the little private brewer and his still at the bottom of the waterfall?'

'Yes, that's right, but it all started long, long ago. Now my brewing friend tells me that they can't make enough to supply the demand.'

They went to the Ford dealer first. They looked at a small Ford Popular and one or two larger models, but Andrew found them very dull. Then they walked through the bazaar to the Morris and Austin Agents. Here Andrew liked a little Austin 7 Ulster. It was a very sporty little two-seater, but it really was extremely small, and Andrew found it difficult to squash his six-foot-plus frame into the driver's seat. They looked at some Morris Eights and these, too, didn't offer any appeal.

They were about to leave, rather disappointed, when the salesman said, 'You seemed to like the Austin Ulster, sir. I have something else which has only just come in and which, I think, may suit you. We only received the car yesterday, and it's in our workshop being washed and polished for the showroom. Please come with me.'

Andrew loved the car immediately. It was an MG J4, a very smart two-seater sports car finished in British Racing Green, with green leather seats. It had full 'all weather' equipment which disappeared from sight when not in use. Andrew fell in love with the car on sight. He turned to the salesman.

'Please tell me about this car,' he said.

'I'll tell you all about the car, sir, and its history, but I must be a little careful and discreet when I come to ownership,' said the salesman. He went on. 'The car is almost new; it's only done four thousand miles, and we imported it for the owner at the end of last year. It's never been in an accident, and we have serviced it from new.'

'Why can't you tell me about the owner?' asked Andrew.

'Well, sir, there has only been one owner, a young planter from Halgranoya, just down the hill there.' He pointed. 'Sadly, the young gentleman got involved with a married lady on the same estate, and the P.D. dismissed him and put him on the first boat to England. He has asked us to sell this car for him.'

'How much are you asking?' enquired Andrew.

'I can show you our books if you like,' said the salesman. 'It cost us nearly seven thousand rupees to bring the car out from England for the young gentleman, and he has asked us to try and get five thousand rupees for him if we can. I can take you out for a run, or I'll let you both take the car out without me – I know Mr Ferguson well – and then, if you like it, perhaps you will tell me if you are interested and would like to make me an offer.'

Andrew drove with Alan beside him and they changed seats for the drive back to the garage. They loved the car and, as Andrew was feeling rich and also feeling sorry for the disgraced owner, he agreed to pay the asking price of five thousand rupees.

The Burgher salesman was waiting for them as they drove into the garage forecourt. 'What do you think of it?' he enquired.

'I think she's marvellous and I'd like to buy her for the five thousand rupees you are asking. There's one small snag though,' Andrew added.

'What's that, sir?' asked de Silva, the salesman.

'Well, it's a matter of money,' said Andrew. 'The position is this. I've only been in Ceylon for a few weeks and I have an account with the Hong Kong Bank in Colombo. Today is Saturday and there's not enough money in my account to pay for the MG. However, I sent the bank a large sterling cheque on Thursday and by Monday it should have been cleared. Once this is done I shall have more than enough to pay for the MG.'

'So what's the problem, sir?' asked de Silva.

'Well, I'd like the car as soon as it's ready, but you may wish to make quite sure the money is in the bank before you give me delivery.'

De Silva thought for a moment. 'Can you give me a cheque now for five thousand rupees?' he asked.

Andrew patted his pocket. 'Yes, I can. I have my cheque book here.'

'When are you going back to Strathmore?' asked de Silva.

'Some time tomorrow evening is the plan.'

'Then there is no problem,' said de Silva. 'I'll start my men cleaning up the MG and checking it thoroughly before servicing it. They'll work for the rest of the day and for as long as necessary on Sunday. As soon as the car is ready I'll deliver it to you, Mr Harvey, at the Grand Hotel. Will you arrange the insurance?'

'Yes,' interrupted Alan, 'we can. Our Agents in Colombo do all that sort of thing. And we must arrange for a Ceylon driving licence for you, too. It's all very simple, Andrew. You go to a police station, a police constable sits beside you in the M.G., you drive around for ten minutes, the PC then says, "Very good, sir," and you get your licence.'

'I didn't realise it was as easy as that,' said Andrew, astonished.

They left the car dealer and made their way to the Golf Club. Andrew turned to Alan. 'The car salesman seemed very fair complexioned. What nationality would he be?'

'He's what is known here as a Burgher. This means that in some past generation there was a marriage between a European and a Singhalese. His name is De Silva and so I suspect that a Portuguese man married a Singhalese woman and so their children, grandchildren, and so on, to the present day, are of mixed blood. The Portuguese came to the island of Ceylon many years ago and more or less took over. It was in the sixteenth century, I believe. Then a hundred years or so later the Dutch arrived and sent the Portuguese packing. Finally, the British took over and sent the Dutch packing. I think the Tamils and the Moorish people too have been here for hundreds of years, but I'm not too sure about that.'

They drove to the Nuwara Eliya Golf Club and had drinks on the verandah overlooking the first tee.

'I haven't been a member here for very long,' said Alan, 'but it's a wonderful course and you can see how well it's kept. If you decide to become a member I'll ask Mr Sanders to propose you. Have you ever played golf at all?'

'Not seriously,' said Andrew. 'I was always too busy with rugger and cricket, but I have hit a few balls from time to time.'

'Well, there's a first class professional here who'll give you a lesson or two if you join. He's a Scot and knows his stuff.'

When they had finished their drinks, the two young men walked over a few holes of the course. Near a stream where the ground was damp, Alan was leading the way when suddenly Andrew saw a blood stain on the light fawn stockings Alan was wearing below his shorts.

'Hey – you're bleeding!' said Andrew.

Alan looked down. 'Oh, a leech,' he said quite calmly, and rolled his stocking down. The revolting creature had not been feeding for too long and was not fully bloated. Nevertheless, it was still a pretty nasty sight.

Andrew immediately inspected his own legs and, to his great relief, found no leeches. 'How do you get that thing off?' he asked Alan.

'Some people burn them off but, as I don't smoke, I'll show you another way – oh look – here's its brother!' he said, pointing to his instep where a leech had left his shoe and was just moving on to his stocking. He pulled it off and showed it to Andrew. 'It's quite safe to pull them off like this before they bite you,' he said, and went on, 'but what you must never do is to try and pull them off once they have got their teeth into you.'

'Why not?' asked Andrew.

'Because then they leave their heads behind, well into your flesh, and the wound festers.'

'What are you going to do?'

'Get some salt from the clubhouse and dab the little brute with that and he'll just fall off, head and all. A lot of golfers carry a little salt in a knot they tie in their handkerchief. As one is always sweating, the salt keeps damp in the hankie and that takes care of leeches for one's round of golf. All you have to do is to dab the leech with the salt and he drops off at once!'

They walked back to the clubhouse and, having removed the leech, they had a delicious curry washed down with more Nuwara Eliya beer. Alan introduced Andrew to several members, some of whom had their wives with them and just one or two had girlfriends. Unmarried young girls were in very short supply in Colombo and up-country.

One married lady seemed to be greatly attracted by Andrew. She had obviously had too many pink gins and had perched on the arm of his chair while they were having their coffee. She was wearing a green cotton dress and a white cardigan. She was smoking and her fingers were badly stained. She was fairly heavily made-up but this did little to hide her wrinkles and rather withered neck.

Alan knew the lady, and her drinking, and other habits all too well. 'We must be getting along Andrew,' he said. 'Perhaps your car has been delivered by now.'

The lady looked cross and stuck her tongue out at Alan. 'Why must you go and spoil things, just as we were getting along so nicely?'

'We really must be going,' said Alan, and Andrew got to his feet.

As they left, Andrew said, 'My M.G. isn't being delivered until tomorrow, Alan. You must remember that?'

'I know it's not,' said Alan, 'but I had to get you away from that harpy. She's poison ivy, and she's caused a lot of trouble in the District. She cottons on to young tea planters even faster than leeches do.'

'Is she anything to do with the owner of my new M.G.? You told me he got into some trouble with someone's wife.'

'No, this is a different woman. The M.G. woman was quite nice; this one is not nice at all. This one's jokingly called "The Black Widow" because she's been through three husbands. People wonder if she eats them. I believe black widow spiders kill their mates and then eat them – not a nice habit.' He went on: 'You know the silly story about the black widow spider who said to her lover "Let's make love in dead Ernest!'

They had a rest in the afternoon and, at tea on the Grand Hotel lawn, Alan said, 'I had a good idea this afternoon. Your M.G. will not be here much before lunch, I imagine. So, if you're feeling really fit, I suggest we climb Pedro in the morning.'

'What's Pedro?' asked Andrew.

'It's the highest point in Ceylon, and it's only two or three miles from here. We call it Pedro, but it's real name is Pidurutalagala. It's a mountain and it's over eight thousand feet high. We drive to the beginning of a track that starts at our height, six thousand one hundred feet, and winds its way through quite thick jungle to the summit. The snag is that we have to leave here at about four in the morning to be at the summit before six to see the sun rise. I've only done it once before but it's very spectacular if it's not a misty or cloudy morning. The view is magnificent and it's all quite beautiful. I've got a torch in the car and we'll get the hotel to prepare some sandwiches and coffee for us to have at the summit. What do you think?'

'I think it's a marvellous idea. I'd love to do it,' said Andrew. 'Are there any snakes or other nasties that we might bump into in the dark?'

Alan laughed. 'No, I don't think so, but the birdsong is really something at daybreak and, if we're lucky, we may even hear a leopard call.'

'Now you *are* scaring me,' said Andrew. 'I'd no idea there were leopards in this area.'

'There are a few and, in fact, a friend of mine called Phillip Fowke had a very nasty experience last year. When we're sitting on the summit tomorrow morning, remind me to tell you the story.'

The two had a quiet dinner together and Alan ordered the sandwiches and coffee for the morning. He also asked for someone to call them at half past three, in case they overslept.

* * *

When they were woken up, they dressed and collected their sandwiches and coffee. Alan was delighted to see a clear sky with bright stars everywhere. 'We're going to be lucky with the weather, Andrew,' he said. 'Let's go.'

After a short drive, they parked at the side of the road and entered some thin jungle at a sign saying 'Pidurutalagala 8282 feet'.

It was a beautiful early morning and although there was a three quarter moon, they needed Alan's torch. Every few yards there was a rough step cut in the path and, to Andrew, the climb seemed endless. Both young men were fit, but the altitude at which they were climbing made them very short of breath. They heard a lot of jungle noises as they climbed: frogs were croaking, cicadas were making their peculiar whirring noise and every now and then they disturbed a bird which took off with a great flapping of wings. Andrew nearly jumped out of his skin on more than one occasion. At last the jungle gave way to patna and they made their way through the rough grass to a small triangle of rocks erected by the Survey Department to mark the summit of the highest point in the island.

Alan and Andrew were in good time and as they flopped down beside the rocky survey point there was just the beginning of a rosy tint in the eastern sky. As they watched, the pink gave way to golden rays and soon after, the sun rose in all its glory. As if to greet the sun, a leopard called some distance from below them. They gazed in silence as the sun lit the countryside, and it was a sight Andrew had never seen before. They had a three hundred and sixty degree view spread out below them. Green tea bushes were everywhere and silver painted tea factories glinted in the early morning sun. They saw a lot of jungle below them and a couple of temples were also visible. There were several lakes and a silver stream wound its way towards the west.

'You were going to tell me about your friend who was attacked by a leopard,' Andrew reminded Alan.

'Oh yes,' said Alan. 'It happened last year on a tea estate called Delmar on the other side of Nuwara Eliya, near the small district of Halgranoya. One of the S.D.s on Delmar was a chap called Phillip Fowke. He and I went to the same school near Bath, a place called Monkton Combe, so I know him pretty well. He is a giant of a man, about six feet four and over fifteen stone, I would say, so you will guess he is pretty strong, which is just as well. To give you some idea of his strength, I remember once being astonished in a car park. Well it wasn't a car park really, it was outside a hotel in Colombo. Phil had a little Austin Seven Ulster like the one we saw yesterday. It was a very smart little two-seater sports car and Phil adored it. Well, someone had parked badly and Phil couldn't reverse out, so he got out of his Austin, went round to the back of the car, picked up the tail with both back wheels off the ground and moved the car so he could reverse out!'

'Wow! A sort of Hercules. What did he do to the leopard, though?'

'He didn't do a lot, actually. Well, not in killing it – but his strength came in when he was fighting for his life. This is what happened. One night Phil's nightwatchman woke him at about four in the morning and said that a coolie had been attacked by a leopard. He went on to say that the coolie was now lying on the factory floor bleeding very badly. Phil was sceptical about it being a leopard that attacked the coolie. He thought it far more likely that the coolie was on his way back to his lines having drunk too much toddy or arrack and had lost his balance and fallen off the narrow estate road into some pruned tea. Anyway, to put up some sort of show Phil put on a pair of slacks and a sweater, loaded his shotgun and drove down to the factory. There was the coolie, very badly injured and bleeding profusely, and the estate doctor was standing by with his car. Phil despatched the man to hospital and asked his teamaker, who had already come down to the factory, what he thought. The teamaker was convinced it was a leopard, and he pointed in the direction where he though the attack may have taken place. Well, Phil thought he really must do something about it, and so he made the teamaker get a lantern and they set off to look for the leopard. The two men walked through the tea until it was just beginning to get light, and by this time Phil was getting pretty fed up with the whole exercise. So, he told the teamaker he'd had enough, gave him his gun to carry and started to walk back to the factory and to his car. Phil told me they hadn't gone a hundred yards when the leopard was on him and he went down like a ninepin, what with the leopard's considerable weight and the power of its charge. They rolled over and over with the leopard's teeth in his shoulder and its back legs trying to disembowel him. He told me that nobody could possibly visualise the terror he felt. He knew he was fighting for his life and he felt, despite his strength, that he was powerless against the leopard's ferocious attack. Just as he was about to pass out he remembered hearing a bang and he woke up in hospital. It seems that the teamaker, poor man, didn't know what on earth to do. He knew he had a loaded shotgun in his hands but with the leopard and his *dorai* rolling over and over in the tea he was frightened of shooting in case he killed Phil and not the leopard. However, when the leopard finally pinned Phil to the ground, and was going for his throat, the teamaker saw his chance. He shoved both barrels up the leopard's backside and pulled both triggers. The leopard was killed on the spot. I've seen the leopard's skin and you can take it from me that it was an enormous beast. Had it not been for Phil's size and strength he would not be planting on Delmar today.

'But what a brave teamaker,' said Andrew.

'Quite so. And the estate gave him a large cheque and arranged quite a party in his honour. Anyway, that's the story – true to the last letter. Now we'll have our sandwiches and coffee and then get back to the hotel. You'll find that the way down is almost as painful as the way up and your knees will feel very stiff tomorrow morning.'

The two young men had hot baths when they returned to the hotel and they were sitting on the front lawn enjoying the morning sun when they heard the M.G. arriving.

Much work had been done on the car since Andrew had seen it the previous day. She gleamed in the sunlight and her chromium plating shone. The driver parked nearby and Andrew and Alan walked over to the car, recognising the driver immediately. It was de Silva.

'How do you think she looks now that she's been washed and polished, sir,' asked de Silva. 'She's had a full service, too,' he added.

'She looks marvellous,' said Andrew. 'How are you going to get back to your showroom?'

'I'm being collected in another car,' said de Silva.

'Good" said Andrew, 'then come over to a table with your papers and we'll complete the deal.'

After lunch Andrew was impatient to drive his new acquisition and they left for Strathmore without delay. Alan led the way and Andrew followed. The journey ended all too soon and a very happy young creeper went to bed that night, thinking how fortunate he was to have acquired such a lovely car at such a reasonable price.

The next morning the two young men were looking at the fresh green leaf that was being weighed on the factory verandah when the Superintendent arrived. 'Ah, I'm glad you're both here,' he said. 'There have been some developments which concern you both. Let's go into the factory office and I'll tell you what's happened.'

They settled themselves, and Mr Sanders began. 'Alan, you'll be disappointed to know that Mark Howell is coming back here. It seems he has not been a great success in his new job, and his P.D. doesn't want him any more, so he's coming back to us. I've managed to postpone things for a month because this means that we must get a bungalow ready for you, Andrew. There's another bungalow available, but it needs some attention. They're starting work today, repainting and doing up the garden and generally making everything presentable, but it will take two or three weeks.'

Peter Sanders went on: 'I see you're looking disappointed, Alan – well, you needn't look sad, because Howell is coming back here in some disgrace and so I've decided to promote you to senior S.D. with Howell as junior S.D. So, Alan, you will move to the senior S.D.'s bungalow, and Howell will go into yours. Andrew will go to the bungalow we're doing up. I'm sorry about all this but perhaps it might only be temporary, we shall just have to wait and see. But I want both of you to make Howell feel as comfortable as possible when he returns. I will have spoken to him before he takes up his duties, but naturally he will not feel particularly happy when I tell him he's been demoted to junior S.D. So I rely on your tact. Anyway, I must be off now. I'll see you both later.'

The Superintendent then left the factory office, and Alan turned to Andrew. 'I'm glad about my promotion of course, Andy, but I'm anything but glad that Howell's coming back. I don't like the man. I don't like his homosexuality either.'

When Andrew had finished his afternoon's work he went back to Alan's bungalow and was delighted to find another letter from Sarah waiting for him. It was a long letter and there was no doubt that she was still deeply in love with him. He admitted to himself that he had not given Sarah the constant thought that he imagined he would when he had left the ship, but then he remembered that he had been pretty fully occupied since he had arrived on Strathmore. However, Sarah's letter brought all the memories of the ship flooding back, and he started his reply that evening. The more he wrote the more he realised how much he loved Sarah. He told her how he longed to see her again and that he dreaded the long wait before this could happen.

Chapter 6

The next three or four weeks seemed to fly by and all too soon Mark Howell arrived back on the estate. As Peter Sanders had expected, Howell was not amused at his return to his old estate, especially as he had been demoted to junior S.D.

By this time Andrew had moved into his new bungalow and Alan had found him a good head boy, who also cooked, and also a second servant. They were both Tamils. Two gardeners appeared and so he was very comfortably installed.

Andrew saw quite a lot of Mark Howell, who seemed remarkably friendly. This was quite a surprise, because Andrew had expected him to be sullen and uncooperative. The only time the two met was during the working day on the estate, but Howell seemed to make a point of chatting to Andrew and laughing and joking with him. However, his attitude to Alan was quite different – it was cold and unfriendly. The antipathy between the two men was clear to see.

About seven o'clock one evening Andrew was lying in a hot bath with a beer on the floor beside him. The door suddenly burst open and Howell stood there. Andrew instinctively looked for his towel to cover himself but Howell was too quick. He kicked the towel away and sat on the edge of the bath.

'My my, you *are* well-built, Andy,' said Howell looking down. 'What are your dimensions?'

'Never mind my dimensions, what are you doing in here? How did you get in?'

'Your boy let me in. He wanted to come in first and warn you that I was here but I wouldn't let him. I thought I'd give you a nice surprise.'

'Well, it's not a nice surprise, you can go and ask Muttiah for a drink and wait for me on the verandah. I'll be with you in a few moments.'

'Oh, come on, Andy, I don't want to see you on the verandah – I like looking at you here. You don't know what a wonderful sight you are. I know, I'll join you in your bath. There won't be too much room

66

for us both, I'm afraid, but we'll manage.' He started undressing.

Andrew was out of the bath in a flash and reached for his towel unsuccessfully. Howell grabbed him and started covering him with kisses. 'I love you, Andy. Please get back in your bath and I'll join you.'

'Get out of here, you filthy bugger. Get out or I'll throw you out.'

Andrew was still quite naked and this inflamed Howell's passion still more.

'Don't be like this, Andy,' Howell pleaded. 'Let me make love to you. I promise you you'll enjoy every minute of it. I've watched you so much in the factory and in the field and I want to be your lover.'

Howell was just under six feet tall and slightly built, and so he was no match for Andrew who grabbed him by the shirt and hurled him into his bedroom. He slammed the bathroom door and wrapped his towel round his waist.

He went back into his bedroom and found Howell sitting on the bed. His face had gone quite pale and he was shaking with rage.

Andrew stood with his back to the bathroom door. 'Get out of my house; get out at once! And if you ever try this on again I'll half kill you.'

'You'll regret this,' snarled Howell. 'You're just as big a prig as Ferguson. You wait until you've been on this estate for a few months with no women you can take to bed, except pluckers. You'll regret having turned me down.'

'Out!' shouted Andrew, 'and remember the warning I've given you. You make me feel quite sick.'

'I'm going, you sanctimonious sod, but you're going to regret this.'

'You're the sod, not me,' said Andrew. 'I'm not a sodomist, now get out.'

It was a few weeks later that the Superintendent had a word with Andrew. He said that one of the most responsible duties a tea planter had was the collection and disbursement of coolie pay. He explained that this had to be ordered from the bank, collected and then paid out to the labour force. It was the duty of the Superintendent to do this but as even a creeper would, one day, be paying his own labour force, it would be a good idea for Andrew to get to know the ropes.

'I'm going to the bank tomorrow,' said Peter, 'so we'll go together, collect the money and then pay it out to the coolies. You and I will sit at the pay table with the head clerk and a Kanakapulle and you can watch what happens. You will see that the money is paid out with the right hand and the coolie takes it with his right hand. Do you know why this should be?'

'No, I don't,' said Andrew.

'Well, you see,' said Peter Sanders, 'the coolies, and others, don't use toilet paper. They wash their bottoms with water using their left hands to do it. So the left hand is considered to be the dirty hand and therefore it is not used for taking things from another person or eating with it or things like that.'

'I'm very glad you told me,' said Andrew. 'I hope I haven't dropped any bricks so far.' He went on: 'What do you do with the money when you have brought it back to the estate and before it is paid out?'

'We keep it in the office safe, and I have the key. When I'm not on the estate the senior S.D. pays the coolies. He has the safe key whilst I'm away.'

At the end of six months Andrew knew all there was to know about coolie pay. It was soon after this that there was a shortage at the pay table. Some three or four hundred rupees were missing. Peter Sanders telephoned the bank at once but the manager assured him that the amount he had collected was correct, and that it had been checked more than once.

The incident was most worrying for the Superintendent, but worse was to come. There was a similar shortage the next month and another the following month. The Superintendent made all the enquiries he could. He had no suspicions; his office staff had been on the estate for many years and nothing like this had ever happened before. Reluctantly he went to the police and, although they were thorough in their investigations, they were no wiser as to who the thief might be.

A week or so later the Superintendent was in Colombo and had, as usual, called on his Colombo Agents. He had finished his business with the senior partner and had made his way over to the young assistant who looked after the insurance business handled by the firm.

This young man knew all about the coolie pay losses on Strathmore because he was handling the claim under the estate's Cash in Transit policy. He said to Peter Sanders, 'I was having dinner in the police officers mess two nights ago. I know most of the young Assistant Superintendents and we have some pretty hilarious parties there from time to time. Well, two evenings ago I met a new young officer. He had come straight from the new crack training school at Hendon and I mentioned your cash shortages to him. He was frightfully keen and said at once, "I can catch the thief." I asked him how he would do this, but he became very cagey and would say no more. He did say, though, that if you could arrange it with his Inspector General he would love to spend two or three days on Strathmore. He would be in plain clothes and he would pretend to be a school friend of one of your S.D.'s.'

'Do you think he could help if he came up to Strathmore?' asked Sanders.

'I was quite impressed by his manner and, anyway, it would do no harm to let him have a go. He might well succeed.'

The visit was arranged and the young police officer was due to arrive on Strathmore two or three days before the next coolie payday.

Soon after Peter Sanders returned to the estate, he saw Mark Howell supervising some clonal work in the nurseries. He came up to the Superintendent and said, 'I wonder if I can have a word with you, sir?'

'What is it Mark?' asked the Superintendent.

'It's about the missing cash. I hate saying this but it's been on my mind so much that I feel I must tell you.'

Peter Sanders dismounted from his horse. 'By all means tell me what you have on your mind, Mark. Why are you worried?'

'Some of the things Andrew has been doing and saying have made me think.'

'Well, that can't have anything to do with missing coolie pay, can it?'

'I don't know,' said Mark. 'First, he comes back with a very expensive new M.G. Then a parcel of rather smart clothes arrives for him from Colombo.'

'Yes,' interrupted the Superintendent, 'but those things happened before the cash started going astray.'

'Yes, I know, but his general appearance, his rather grand manner. He tells me he's going to get engaged to, and then marry, the daughter of the owner of a large steamship line. He's very generous at buying drinks at the club. I could not afford any of these things when I was a creeper, and my intuition says that Master Andrew may be at the bottom of the mystery. He's been going with you quite often to collect the coolie pay, and perhaps there have been moments when he could have put his hand into the bag.'

'I don't think so and, anyway, once it's in the safe I'm the only one who has the key. I would need some definite evidence, some very definite evidence indeed, before I approached Andrew.'

'Yes, I quite understand, sir, it's just this very strong feeling I have.

I suppose you wouldn't agree to his bungalow being searched?'

'No, I certainly would not. You can forget the whole thing.' Sanders remounted and rode away. On arrival at the estate office he saw his head clerk in conversation with a figure in a white shirt and a white sarong.

On seeing the Superintendent, Chidambaram, the clerk, came out to meet him. He was carrying a thick woollen sock.

He salaamed the Superintendent and said, 'This is quite a shock, sir. This is Harvey *dorai*'s house boy. Harvey *dorai* saw some white ants in his cupboard yesterday and told Muttiah here to take everything out of the cupboard and give it a good scrubbing. While doing this Muttiah pulled out this sock from under some clothes in the bottom drawer. Look sir, it's full of money, our missing coolie pay, perhaps. Muttiah did not know what to do but he knows about the coolie pay doing a bunk and so he thought he had better tell *Dorai*.'

Peter Sanders walked away, his hand to his head, trying to collect his thoughts. At first he was too shocked and saddened to think straight. How could Andrew have done this? He went back to the two men.

'Tell Muttiah to go back to Harvey *dorai*'s bungalow and to put the sock back exactly where he found it. Tell him to finish cleaning the cupboard and put all the clothes and things back as they were before. And Chidambaram, listen to me: neither you nor Muttiah are to say a word about this to anyone, to *anyone at all*, do you understand? If one word gets out I'll skin the pair of you alive. Now, off you go and not a word to anyone.'

Sanders rode back to his own bungalow for lunch and to meet the young policeman who was almost due. Alan Ferguson was already there and puzzled at being invited to lunch with the P.D. on a week day.

The first thing the P.D. did was to excuse himself, and took his wife aside, whereupon he told her briefly what Mark Howell had just told him. Then, making sure he did not tell Howell's story to Alan, the Superintendent took Alan into his confidence with regard to the pending arrival of the policeman from Colombo. He went on to say that the young officer was newly arrived from Hendon and that he, the officer, was confident he could catch the thief who was stealing the coolie pay. He told Alan that the young man's name was John Manning, that he would be in plain clothes and that he would pretend to be an old school friend of Alan's, and was spending a short holiday in Ceylon. He said nothing about the cash found in Andrew's wardrobe.

They had just started on a drink before lunch when Muttusamy brought the Buick to rest under the porch. A fresh-faced young man got out of the front passenger's seat and walked round the bonnet of the car. He was of medium height, slim with very fair hair.

'I'm John Manning, sir,' he said to the Superintendent, and they shook hands.

'You're very welcome, Mr Manning,' said Peter Sanders. 'This business of stolen coolie pay is very worrying. We're insured, of course, so it's not so much the loss of the money, it's more not knowing who is taking it that's disturbing.' He introduced the policeman to Mrs Sanders and Alan.

Mrs Sanders took Manning away so that he could freshen himself up after the long drive from Colombo. 'When did Muttusamy pick you up this morning?' she asked.

'Fairly early, just after six o'clock. We had a brief stop in Kandy. It was the most attractive drive. I've never been to Ceylon before.'

They moved into lunch and, once they had been served, the servants withdrew and Sanders turned to the young officer. 'Can you tell us a little bit about how you are going to go about catching this thief?' he asked.

'Very little at present, but once I have caught him – and I *will* catch him – then I'll be delighted to tell you more. But for now I must ask you some questions.'

'Please do,' said Sanders. 'We're ready to give you all the help we can.'

'Good, then here goes. First, when are you going to collect the next lot of pay? Is it tomorrow morning? That's what I was told in Colombo.'

'Yes, I'll be at the bank by ten o'clock or so, and I shall bring the money back here and lock it in our safe.'

'And when will you pay it out?'

'The day after tomorrow.'

'Good,' said Manning. 'That will give me enough time to do certain things I have to do in the three days I have here before I go back to Colombo. But the point is this. For my plan to work the thief must act tomorrow night. If he doesn't, and you find no shortage when you pay your labour force, then I'll have to come back next month and have another go. You may have to get permission from Colombo for me to do this. Can I come with you to the bank tomorrow morning?'

Sanders laughed. 'Do you suspect that I may steal some of the money on the way back here?'

'No, of course not. It's just that I'd love to have a drive to Nuwara Eliya and back!'

'Good,' said Sanders, 'then I'll pick you up at Ferguson's bungalow at nine tomorrow morning.'

When the Superintendent and his wife were left alone, Mrs Sanders turned to her husband. 'Do you think that that young man is going to catch his thief? I'll be so glad and relieved, darling, when this whole horrible affair is over. I cannot believe Andrew is the culprit. I cannot believe he would steal and, anyway, how can he break into the office safe? There's only one key, and you keep it. Andrew is too nice a boy to do such a thing.'

'There's some pretty damning evidence against him,' said Sanders. 'How did the money find its way into his sock? Well, we'll just have to wait and see what Manning produces.'

The Superintendent and the young police officer had a pleasant drive to the bank the next morning, collecting the coolie pay and returning to Strathmore without delay.

As they went into the Superintendent's office, Manning said, 'Now sir, please do exactly as I say. Please give me the cash and your safe key. Then please leave me alone in this office for fifteen minutes and, in that time, please talk to your staff in the outer office. Please keep them occupied until you return to your own office in fifteen minutes. Tell them any story you like to allay their suspicions as to what I could be doing in your private office.'

'That's asking rather a lot, Mr Manning,' said Peter Sanders. 'Why can't I stay with you whilst you're doing whatever you are going to do?'

'If you really feel you must, then I'll have to agree. The thing is that what I'm going to do is something I've brought out from Hendon and it's rather hush-hush at present.'

'I understand. I'll come back here in fifteen minutes. Here's the safe key.'

Manning was staring out of the office window when the Superintendent returned. He turned and smiled at Sanders. 'All done, sir. Here's your key and now we must wait and hope there's a burglary!'

Andrew, Alan and John Manning drove to the Radella Club that evening and Alan waved to a rather sulky looking Mark Howell standing in his garden as they passed. They had drinks and a meal at the club before driving home again in bright moonlight.

The next afternoon a chair was provided for Manning at the pay table and paying the labour force began. To the policeman's delight there was a shortage of three hundred and eighty rupees.

Manning moved over to the Superintendent. 'All the coolies can go,' he said, 'but I want your clerks and those factory workers of "clerk" category here. I also want your doctor, your teacher and anyone else of similar rank here as soon as possible.'

The Superintendent nodded to his head clerk who went to the office telephone to get the doctor and the others. It took about twenty minutes before everyone was assembled and, during that time, John Manning said nothing and continued to sit on his chair. Peter Sanders looked at him in puzzlement, but Manning just shook his head and said nothing.

A car arrived and Sanders said, 'Right, now we're all here. What do we do next?'

Manning got up. 'First, I want all the Europeans in front of me.' They looked at each other with raised eyebrows, but did what the policeman had asked. 'Now show me the palms of your hands,' he said. He went along the line and inspected the show of hands. He turned to Sanders. 'Please ask these other gentlemen to do the same. I do not want to see the hands of those gentlemen who actually paid out the money.'

The head clerk asked the others to hold out their palms.

Manning did his inspection and turned away slowly shaking his head in disappointment and disbelief. 'There's someone missing. Who's not here, sir?' he asked.

'Only one of my junior S.D.s, a young man called Mark Howell who reported sick this morning,' said Sanders.

'Where is he now?' asked Manning.

'In his bungalow, I imagine.'

'Then let's go there and see him,' said the policeman.

'How did you know someone was missing from the pay table?' asked Sanders.

'I hope very much you'll see for yourself in a few moments,' said Manning.

Muttusamy and the Buick were close by and Sanders, his creeper and S.D., together with John Manning, piled in. 'Muttusamy, please drive us to Howell *dorai*'s bungalow,' said Sanders.

They found Howell sitting on his verandah reading a magazine. He got up and walked to the front steps when he recognised his Superintendent.

'How are you feeling, Mark?' asked Sanders, and introduced John Manning. Manning put out his hand and, after a moment's hesitation, Howell took it.

'Your palm and fingers are bright green, Mr Howell. How do you account for that?' asked Manning.

Howell looked ready to faint. He sat down.

'I am an assistant superintendent of police,' said Manning. He walked up to Howell. 'I'm arresting you, Howell, on a charge of stealing, other charges may follow when I know more about you.' He gave Howell the usual formal warning and then turned to Peter Sanders.

'I'll give this man some time to put some clothes together while I wait. Will you please send your car and driver back here as soon as he's dropped you at your house? I shall be taking my prisoner to the Nuwara Eliya police station where they will lock him up for the night. I'd like either Alan or Andrew to accompany us in case Howell tries any funny stuff on the way to Nuwara Eliya.'

There was a violent disturbance as Howell rushed at Andrew. He looked like a madman, his face was working with hatred as he lunged at the creeper. Manning was too quick for him and had him in a half-Nelson lock in a flash.

'You bastard,' Howell yelled, trying again to get at Andrew. 'You bloody prig, I'll get you one day. I'll teach you not to deny me again. You wait!'

'Listen to me, Howell,' said Manning. 'I've no handcuffs with me but any more nonsense from you and I'll tie you up. I'll also add assault to the charges I'm going to bring against you.'

Before Sanders left in the Buick, he said to Alan, 'We'll all dine at my bungalow this evening, and then Manning can tell us as many of his secrets as he is allowed to. Come along about eight o'clock.'

The policeman had no trouble with his prisoner and Howell was put in a police cell in Nuwara Eliya. On the way back, Manning told Andrew that he was feeling rather pleased with himself and was looking forward to dinner with the Superintendent and his wife that evening.

When the party had gathered in the drawing room, John Manning was surprised to see a roaring fire in the grate. He then remembered that the evenings at five or six thousand feet were quite cold.

When drinks had been served, Peter Sanders said, 'Now John, put us in the picture. Tell us how you managed to trap Howell.'

'I can only tell you so much because the method is new and we don't want the criminal fraternity to know how we work. However, I can say this. It was obvious that the thief would have to go to the safe himself and handle the money. There was a hundred to one chance that he might be wearing gloves but I felt sure he would have bare hands. I therefore dusted the coins lightly with a powder that we have developed at Hendon. The ingredients are secret but I can say that we have an element of copper sulphate in the mixture that turns the hands green. Your coolies will be wondering why they all have green hands! The rest you know, but I ask you most seriously to treat all I've said in the strictest confidence.'

'Of course we will,' said Sanders, 'but why on earth would Howell want to steal and, anyway, how did he get a key to the safe?'

'He had a duplicate, that's obvious,' said Manning, 'and, when I question him, before charging him officially, I'll try and find out how and when he got a duplicate.'

'I don't think you need question Howell about the matter of the key,' said Sanders after a moment's thought. 'You see, he was my Senior S.D. and so when I was away he used to pay the labour force and so he had the safe key. He could easily have had a duplicate made.'

'Why on earth did he do it?' said Angela Sanders. 'Mark wasn't exactly the nicest character, but to stoop to stealing, that's something I can't understand.'

'I've had some time to think, and I believe I know the complete answer,' said Andrew.

The others looked at him in surprise.

John Manning was the first to react. 'Tell us at once, please. What you have to say could be of vital importance to me. I've caught the thief but I don't know why he embarked on a series of thefts.'

'It all stems from one fact,' said Andrew. 'Mark is a homosexual.'

The others stared at him.

'Go on,' said Manning.

'Soon after I moved into my new bungalow, I had a visit from Mark. I was having a bath at about seven one evening before changing for dinner when Mark burst into the bathroom. I grabbed at my towel, which was on the floor beside me, but he kicked it out of the way. He started taking off his clothes and he said he was going to join me in the bath because he wanted to make love to me. I was horrified and I told him to get out. We had a scuffle and, as I am a bigger man than he is, I won the fight. I told Howell if he didn't go I would throw him out. His loving mood changed abruptly and he started screaming obscenities at me. He finished up by saying I would regret having rebuffed him.'

Andrew went on: 'Mark knew that Mr Sanders was teaching me how to collect coolie pay. He knew I went with the P.D. to collect it, and he saw I was at the pay table when it was paid out. He felt he would get his revenge if I was suspected of stealing some of it. After all, I was the obvious suspect. I'm sure I'm right.'

There was a silence, and then Peter Sanders said quietly, 'Yes, I'm quite sure you're right, even more sure than you are because there are two things you don't know, Andrew. First, Mark has already told me that he thought you were stealing the money. I asked him why he suspected you. He said because you had an expensive car, good clothes, that you were generous with your money and that he could never have afforded such things when he was a creeper.'

'Then,' the Superintendent continued, 'my adverse reaction to Mark's theory that you were the thief didn't please him, so he did a quite despicable thing. He managed to hide quite a lot of stolen money in one of your socks. He then put the sock full of money under some clothes in your cupboard. Muttiah, your boy, found it and brought it to me.'

'Well, thank you very much,' said Manning. 'That completes my case for me. I'm very grateful.'

'How awful,' said Angela. 'What will they do with Mark?'

'He'll go to jail. It's a cut and dried case,' said Manning. 'If you don't want him to go to Welikade, the Colombo jail – which is not very nice, I'm told – you could plead for him to be deported to England.'

They moved into dinner in shocked silence. Mrs Sanders was the first to speak when they had all sat down. 'I'm so glad that Mark's efforts to incriminate Andrew have failed. To go to the lengths of hiding money in Andrew's socks is quite dreadful. I'm very glad he's been caught. There's no knowing what he might have done next.' She turned to Andrew. 'How do you feel now, Andrew? You must be relieved to know that it's all over.'

'In a way, yes,' said Andrew, 'but had I known that I had been under suspicion, I would really be feeling relieved now. I think the thing I will never forget is the look of hatred on Mark's face as he lunged at me. His face was contorted in a rictus – if that is the word – of malevolence and hatred. He almost looked rabid to me.'

'Well, it's all over now, Andrew,' said Peter Sanders. 'There was evidence against you, I know, but somehow I couldn't possibly suspect you. At the same time I had no idea that Mark was the culprit.'

Almost by tacit mutual agreement, it was decided that the matter should be left to rest there, and everyone put their minds to enjoying a pleasant evening at the Superintendent's residence.

A few days later the Superintendent summoned his S.D. and his creeper to his office. 'It seems,' he said, 'that Nankawella factory, up the road, was destroyed by fire last night. Macaulay, the Superintendent, has rung me to see if I can make his green leaf for him while his factory is being rebuilt. He's desperate to find a top factory like ours to come to his rescue, because his Nankawella teas are pretty good. I'd like to help him if I can, but before I ring Colombo, I thought I'd like to discuss the pros and cons with you two. Do you think our factory can handle this extra green leaf?'

Alan said, 'Off the cuff I think it can, because Nankawella is smaller than we are and, with our new driers and rollers, I'm sure we can handle Macaulay's leaf.'

'I'm rather lost, sir,' said Andrew. 'I haven't Alan's experience, and it would be extremely difficult for me to comment, only having been out here for such a comparatively short time.'

'Of course you can't,' said Peter Sanders. 'Let me explain. Nankawella tea factory has been destroyed by fire. This means that the green leaf will go on growing on the bushes but there will be nowhere for it to be turned into black tea, because now there is no factory. So the P.D. is searching around the district for a friendly factory to help him out. He has come to us because he knows that our Strathmore teas do very well on the market and therefore we would be able to manufacture his green leaf to the same standards as our own.'

'I see,' said Andrew. 'Do we lump Mr Macaulay's green leaf with our own, or do we manufacture his leaf separately?'

'Good question, Andrew. I think almost certainly we lump it in with our own leaf, but it will depend on the quality of the leaf when it arrives at our factory. I mean, if the plucking has been coarse I would reject the leaf and tell Macaulay why. I'm not having stalk in my teas. Anyway, I must first find out if Colombo agrees to our helping out.'

The Strathmore Agents in Colombo made sure from Peter Sanders that they had the capacity to handle the Nankawella leaf, and then they agreed that Strathmore should help the unfortunate Macaulay. Terms were discussed and agreed.

Sanders sent for Andrew and they met in the factory. 'I want you to be responsible for the success of the new arrangement, Andrew,' said the P.D., and he went on: 'I'll explain what will happen, and I'll give you some idea of the snags and pitfalls you'll have to look out for. The first thing to remember is that Nankawella is insured under what is known as a Loss of Profits policy. This insures any losses the estate company may suffer as a result of the factory being destroyed by fire. Now, apart from the extra expenditure they will incur in sending their green leaf here, and paying our fees for making their tea, they will also suffer a loss in tea. In fact it will only be a loss of water. Sounds ridiculous, doesn't it?'

'I don't understand,' said Andrew.

'No, of course you don't. Why should you? But I'm at an advantage here. You see, when I was an S.D., the estate I was on lost their factory in a fire and I was responsible for sending our green leaf to another factory. In sending our leaf I would put, say, five thousand pounds of our green leaf into our estate lorry and send it off to the friendly factory for manufacture. When the green leaf got there the Kanakapulle would weigh it and he would find, say, a ten per cent shortage in weight, say four thousand five hundred pounds weight instead of the five thousand pounds I put into the lorry. What had happened was the leaf had already started withering in the hot lorry on the hot journey to the other factory. In fact all that was lost was, as I say, moisture or water. And, in any case, as soon as the green leaf was unloaded it would be taken up to the withering lofts and the withering process would continue. But here's the snag. Had I manufactured five thousand pounds of green leaf in my own factory I would have got about one thousand one hundred and fifty pounds of black tea, say twenty-three per cent. But the friendly factory didn't get five thousand pounds of leaf. They only got four thousand five hundred pounds because ten per cent had withered on the way over. So instead of getting his one thousand one hundred and fifty pounds of black tea, the friendly superintendent only got twenty-three per cent of four thousand five hundred pounds, or say a little over one thousand pounds – I can't work out the exact percentages in my head. Now our insurance company refused to pay our claim because they said we had only lost water. In the end we convinced them that the end result was a loss of black tea and so they paid!'

Andrew frowned, but then said, 'I think I understand, sir.'

'Don't worry,' said the P.D. 'You'll soon get the hang of it. The thing to remember, though, is to give the Nankawella lorry driver a receipt for the actual poundage of green leaf he delivers at the factory door. Oh, and of course see that it is well-plucked leaf – no stalks, because don't forget it is going to be lumped in with our leaf.'

'How long will this new arrangement last?' asked Andrew.

'Until the new factory has been built on Nankawella – I would say between a year and a half and two years. The loss of profits policy usually has an indemnity period of between eighteen and twenty-four months.'

That evening Andrew was due to have his Tamil lesson from Murugiah, the schoolmaster. He heard the ancient motorcycle struggling up the hill and he moved out onto the verandah to greet his old friend.

In the middle of the lesson Murugiah paused and looked at Andrew. 'A bad show, sir, about the factory fire on Nankawella. We are going to manufacture their green leaf, I am told.'

'Yes, that's right,' said Andrew, 'and our P.D. has put me in charge of the arrangement.'

'Do you know how the fire started, sir?' asked Murugiah.

'No, I don't. Do you?'

'Well, I can only tell you what I have heard. You know, sir, I am friends with the schoolmaster on Nankawella, and he and I were talking the other evening. He tells me that the fire was deliberately started.'

'You shouldn't be telling me such things, Murugiah, unless you are quite sure of your facts,' said Andrew.

'I am only telling you, sir, because I think you should tell Sanders *dorai* and he will know what to do with the information. It's important, sir, but please don't tell Sanders *dorai* that I told you.'

Andrew was thoroughly intrigued by now. 'Go on, Murugiah, tell me the whole story and you can rely on my discretion as to what I tell the P.D.'

'Well, sir, it seems that a factory Kanakapulle on Nankawella has been making eyes at another Kanakapulle's wife. She is enjoying this and is having high jinks with that Kanakapulle. Therefore she is neglecting her husband and not cooking his rice properly. She is also giving him the cold shoulder!'

'Go on,' said Andrew, trying hard not to smile.

'So, the one Kanakapulle is wondering how to have revenge on the other Kanakapulle. So he thinks he will put that Kanakapulle out of a job by setting fire to the factory so that there will be no factory work for the Kanakapulle. The silly fool is not realising he is putting himself out of a job also. That is the talk on the estate, sir.'

It took Andrew a little time to figure out which Kanakapulle did what. He said, 'You did right in telling me, Murugiah. I must tell Sanders *dorai* because it might affect the insurance policy.'

When Andrew told his P.D. about his chat with Murugiah, he took it quite calmly. 'You remember that I told you about this sort of thing on your first visit to the factory. There's a lot of jealousy about,

Andrew,' he said, 'and in serious cases the aggrieved one takes revenge on the one responsible. We can leave this in the capable hands of the Nankawella P.D. He'll know all about it already, no doubt, and he'll know what to do. In any case, the Nankawella insurance policy will cover malicious damage'.

Chapter 7

Word of Andrew's prowess at rugger had filtered through to the 'Up Country' rugger enthusiasts and he was telephoned one evening in his bungalow. He was invited to play in a game the following Saturday. He did quite well in the game, but soon realised he was not quite as fit as he used to be. He felt better when someone at the club told him that he should remember he had been playing at a height of over 5000 feet, and it was not surprising he felt short of breath.

Whilst they were having drinks at the bar, after they had changed, Andrew found himself talking to a young Ceylonese player who had come up to him and taken a seat by his side. 'My name is Coswatte,' he said, and he went on, 'I'm creeping on an estate on the far side of Nuwara Eliya, in a district called Udapussellawa. I think you're creeping too?'

'Yes, I'm on Strathmore, and I love it,' replied Andrew. 'I like the estate, the people I work with, the climate – in fact, I love the whole island of Ceylon or, at least, those parts I've seen of it. I haven't seen very much yet, but I'm going to use any local leave I get in touring the island.'

'I'm glad to hear you say that you love Ceylon,' said Coswatte, 'because I, too, love my island. I'm a Kandyan, which means I come from Kandy and my ancestors go back a long way. In fact, I believe I'm descended from the ancient Kandyan kings. That sounds as if I'm bragging, but I'm not. I believe and hope it's a fact.'

'I don't think you're bragging at all,' said Andrew. 'I wouldn't mind being descended from a king or two, but my ancestors were only merchants in the City of London. Although one of my mother's relations was Lord Mayor of London a long time ago.'

'His name wasn't Whittington, and he didn't have a cat, I suppose?' asked Coswatte, smiling.

'Well done!' said Andrew. 'You know your English fairy tales, I see.'

He grinned. 'Yes, some of them. I have an idea,' said Coswatte. 'By the way, my name is Mahinda, although my friends call me Patrick. Please call me Patrick, if you like.'

'Yes, I will, Patrick. Thanks,' said Andrew. 'What's your idea?'

'Well, in July or August every year, they have an enormous procession of elephants and dancers who go through the streets of Kandy after dark. It's a wonderful sight, because the elephants, over a hundred, usually, are all gaudily dressed-up in what looks like silks and jewels, and they are surrounded by drummers and dancers. These, too, are wonderfully dressed in historic Kandyan costumes. Others in the procession carry flaming torches. It's a sight one has to see for oneself, to fully appreciate the grandness of it all.'

'How does one get to see a sight like that?' asked Andrew.

'Well – and this is my idea – if you're interested, and if you can get a weekend's leave, I can arrange everything.'

Andrew settled himself on his bar stool. 'Please tell me more, Patrick. I really am interested.'

'The procession is part of what we Kandyans call our "Pera Hera",' said Patrick. 'Every July or August, according to the time of the full moon, we have our Pera Hera. The object of the procession is to carry the relic of the Sacred Tooth around the streets of Kandy so that all the people can see it and worship it. The legend of the Sacred Tooth goes back a long way. It is said that it is the tooth of the Lord Buddha, and it has been worshipped for hundreds of years. It is now carried on one of the first elephants, a huge beast with the most gorgeous gold and blue trappings. It is usually the largest tusker in the procession, and the relic is carried in a gold casket. There are drummers and musicians playing pipes, people cracking whips and others letting off fireworks. There are so many flaming torches it is like daylight, and you can see everything very clearly. In front of the procession are various Kandyan dignitaries in national costume. These costumes are very grand, and on their tops they wear short, gold, richly embroidered jackets, and below there are yards and yards of white material in the form of a very large sarong. My father used to take part in the procession, and I know it took him hours and hours to dress.'

'It all sounds fascinating,' said Andrew. 'I'd simply love to see your Pera Hera. Will you make the necessary arrangements, or can I help you? I must certainly pay my share of all the expenses.'

'Please leave it all to me,' said Patrick. 'It's very easy, really. You see, my parents live just outside Kandy. They will put us up and so there will be no expenses for accommodation. A lot of people book front rooms in the Queens Hotel and watch the procession from there. That's all very well, but I think you and I should watch it from the street and mingle with the crowd. You will get a much more vivid impression, a far stronger feeling of excitement if we're right in the middle of things. The noise, the smell, the lot! I recommend it.'

'You're the expert, Patrick. Please go ahead and make the arrangements. It's very kind of you to give me such a treat. Please give me as much notice as you can so that I can get some leave.'

While the two men had been talking, Andrew had noticed a good-looking woman standing with her young daughter a little distance from the bar. When Patrick had left, Andrew went over to her and introduced himself.

'I'm glad you've come over,' she said, 'because my daughter thinks you're terrific!'

'Oh Mum!' said the girl, blushing furiously.

Her mother put her arm round her shoulder and looked at Andrew. 'I don't blame Valerie,' she said. 'You certainly are a very good-looking young man. Are you from this district?'

'My name is Andrew Harvey, and I'm creeping on Strathmore. I haven't been in Ceylon very long.'

'Oh,' said the lady. 'Well, my daughter is only sixteen but I have told her there is very little point in her hoping one day . . .' She stopped and looked down at her feet with an expression of embarrassment.

'That's right, I'm afraid,' said Andrew. 'I have a girlfriend with whom I'm very much in love. I met her on the boat coming out, and I hope to marry her in five years' time when my first agreement is over.'

'But I thought – er . . .' The lady looked more embarrassed than ever.

'What is it you want to say?' asked Andrew.

'Oh, nothing.'

'But I'm sure there is. You've stopped short in mid-sentence twice now. Please tell me what you were going to say.'

'Please, I'd rather not. We must find my husband; it's high time we left.'

Andrew took her by the arm. 'You simply must tell me. I'm really worried now. You know something about me and you're embarrassed about telling me. Please, what is it? I must know.'

'Valerie, go and find Dad and say that I'll be with you both in a moment.' She turned to Andrew. 'This is awful, I feel such a fool. I will tell you, but will you be very kind and promise you will not tell anyone about my stupidity?'

'I don't know who you are, so I can't cause you any embarrassment – in any case, I wouldn't want to – but I promise not to involve you in any way. Now, what is it? What's making you so embarrassed?'

'Well, I'm surprised you have a girlfriend. You see, the story in the district is that you don't like young girls very much, that you – er – prefer young men. I hope that that's not true. I hope it's only a nasty rumour.'

'I can assure you that it is by no means true. I can go further and tell you that I have a very good idea who started this horrible rumour. Please believe me when I say I'm quite normal. I have no homosexual tendencies and I hope, one day, you'll meet my wife-to-be. I must tell my P.D. about this rumour but I promise I won't mention you. I'll just say "someone" brought up the subject. My P.D. knows the whole story and he will take appropriate action.'

The lady put her arm on Andrew's and kissed him lightly on the cheek. 'Thank you for being so kind,' she said, and hurried away.

The next morning Andrew went up to the big bungalow and found the P.D. and Mrs Sanders having breakfast on the verandah. 'Hello, Andrew,' said Mrs Sanders, 'we're having a leisurely late breakfast because it's Sunday. Come and have a cup of coffee.'

Andrew sat down. 'Thanks, Mrs Sanders. I'm so glad you're here too, because there's something that's worrying me and I'd like to tell you both what it's all about.'

'Carry on, Andrew,' said the P.D.

'Well, I was playing rugger yesterday at Dimbula and, after the match, I found myself talking to a lady and her sixteen-year-old daughter. The lady was talking to me and suddenly she went very quiet and was obviously embarrassed by something or other. She wouldn't tell me what it was at first but, in the end, I managed to persuade her to reveal what was troubling her. She said that the talk in her district was that I was a homosexual, that I had no use for girls and that I preferred boys instead. So I told her about Sarah Allenby, whom I met on the boat coming out, and I said I hoped to marry her one day.'

Andrew went on: 'I've had all night to think about this, and I'm sure it's Mark Howell trying to get his own back on me. What can I do, sir?'

'Nothing, nothing at all,' said the P.D. 'Neither Angela nor I have heard any talk of this sort about you. Yes, I'm quite sure Howell is behind the gossip. He's in jail now, so he can't do any more harm, but don't worry, Andrew, we'll make it our business to scotch this dreadful rumour. It would be nice if Sarah could visit you here one day – that would really put paid to this wicked talk.'

Angela Sanders had sent for an extra coffee cup while her husband had been talking. She filled this and drew up her chair close to Andrew's. She put her arm over his shoulder. 'If you were my son, Andy, I'd be in tears by now – I very nearly am, anyway. You poor boy. You've had nothing but bad luck ever since you've been on Strathmore, and I know that Mark Howell has been at the bottom of it.'

'In more ways than one!' murmured Peter Sanders, winking at Andrew.

'That's enough of that, Peter,' said Mrs Sanders, 'although I might have put that last sentence more tactfully.' She turned back to Andrew. 'My husband said just now that it would be nice if Sarah could pay you a visit. Well, why not? 'You've had a very rough time since you've been here, and I think a visit from Sarah would act like a tonic. We'd be delighted if she stayed with us here in the big bungalow for a few weeks. I know Peter is very pleased indeed, and impressed, with your work, particularly as you've had so much personal worry and anxiety which could have distracted you. So think about it, Andy.'

'I don't need to. Are you quite sure, Mrs Sanders, that you'd let Sarah stay with you for a little while? What a marvellous thought – I feel as if I'd just won a fortune. If you're quite sure, can I write to Sarah today?'

'Why not telegraph her?' said the P.D.

Andrew paused. 'I think I'll write, sir,' he said. 'There's so much I want to tell her and it won't all go into a telegram. Sarah's going to get the shock of her life. I'll certainly ask her to telegraph her reply to me. How very, very kind of you both.' He got up to go.

'Just a moment, Andrew,' said Peter Sanders. 'There's something I've been meaning to tell you for a day or two now, but it keeps on slipping my mind. Our estate doctor leaves us today. He's sixty-five now, and is due to retire. A much younger man is taking his place and is moving in some time this afternoon. You might look in on him this evening to see that he's got everything he wants. Ask him too, if he's been shown the hospital and crèche and if he's happy about everything. Tell him I'll see him tomorrow.'

'I'll do that, sir,' said Andrew. He grinned. 'I must hurry away. I have a long letter to write to someone I know in England. Someone who's got a two week sea voyage in front of her, although she doesn't know that yet! Mrs Sanders, I'm not dreaming, am I?'

'No, you're not, Andrew. Off you go, and write that letter!'

When Andrew had reversed the M.G. and had left, Mrs Sanders turned to her husband. 'We've made one young man very happy, I think. It was a brainwave of yours, Peter, to suggest Sarah should visit Strathmore. I don't think Andrew is going to give Mark Howell and his evil ways another thought.'

On arriving at his bungalow, Andrew was greeted by his servant who said that Patrick Coswatte had telephoned and would Andrew ring him back.

Andrew put a call through at once and Coswatte answered. 'Andrew, my parents would be delighted if you and I could stay with them this coming weekend. It's full moon and the Pera Hera should be at its best. Can you make it? I can pick you up on Saturday morning – it's on my way to Kandy – and I'll drop you back on Sunday evening.'

'Yes, you bet I can make it! But look, I've just got a newish M.G. and I'm longing to give her a long run. If you'll come here on Saturday morning, you can leave your car in my garage and we'll go to Kandy and back in the M.G. How very kind of your parents. Please thank them and say I am delighted to accept.'

Andrew wrote to Sarah telling her at some length about the Sanders' invitation for her to spend a few weeks with them on Strathmore. He asked her to telegraph her reply, and then dropped the letter in the tappal bag for posting in the morning.

At six o'clock that evening he drove up to the estate hospital to meet the new doctor. He wondered what he would be like. He imagined a youngish man, small and slim, with spectacles and probably a stethoscope round his neck. He couldn't have been more wrong.

A tall slim figure was standing on the hospital steps talking to an orderly wearing a white apron. The figure turned when he heard the M.G., dismissed the orderly, and walked slowly towards the car. As Andrew stopped the car he had a brief moment to inspect the new doctor. He saw a very dark man, about six feet tall, with the figure of an athlete. The shoulders were broad, the waist slim and the white drill suit couldn't be faulted. Andrew hauled himself out of the M.G. and the doctor came round the car to meet him, hand outstretched.

'My name is Mervyn Coomasaru. I'm the new doctor,' he said. The two men shook hands.

'And my name is Andrew Harvey and I'm a creeper on Strathmore.

I've come to welcome you and to make sure you have everything you want. The superintendent, Mr Sanders, will see you tomorrow morning.'

'Well, thank you,' said Coomasaru. 'I have been shown around the hospital and the crèche, and everything seems fine. I have a plucker in here at the moment and I expect her to go into labour in a few hours' time. I've warned the orderly to stand by.'

Andrew had time to look at the new doctor while he was talking. He was nothing like the figure he had expected to see. The man was very dark-skinned and the eyes were quite unusual. They were a dark golden yellow, and were a striking and compelling feature. He was good-looking beyond the ordinary, almost film-star quality, and to his handsomeness was added an air of self assurance not usually found in a man still in his twenties. The features were firm and angular with no trace of coarseness. The man stood erect and held his head high.

'Have you worked on a tea or other estate before?' asked Andrew.

'Yes, on tea and rubber estates, but not for very long, only a year or two. I lived in England for about twelve years. After I left Oxford I trained in London and, when that was over, I became a doctor. A little while ago I came out to see some relations I have here. These relations had a rubber estate in the Kelani Valley and I worked in the estate hospital for four or five months and that was my first job in Ceylon. Quite recently I heard about this vacancy on Strathmore.'

'Did you go to school in England?'

'Yes, I went to Cheltenham.'

'I asked because your English is so good.' said Andrew.

'Well, thank you, but now I shall have to brush up on my Tamil and my Singhalese. They're practically non-existent.'

'Do you propose to make a career of your work as a doctor on a tea estate for the rest of your life? Forgive me for asking so many personal questions but, to put it plainly, you're not at all the sort of chap I expected to see.'

Coomasaru laughed. 'I'll take that as a compliment but, to answer your question, I think the answer is probably no. It's hard to be definite, but who knows? I may like this work so much that I may stay on if I'm asked to.'

'My bungalow is down the hill, and the estate switchboard will put you through. Please don't hesitate to ring me if there is anything you want.'

Andrew drove away puzzled. This Adonis of a doctor was not at all what he had expected. He thought the new medical officer would have no shortage of lady pluckers once they discovered who was to look after them in hospital.

The day that Andrew and Patrick Coswatte were due to leave for Kandy and the Pera Hera was perfect in every way. When Patrick arrived at Andrew's bungalow at about ten in the morning, the sun was shining in a cloudless sky over hundreds of acres of emerald-green tea bushes spread over the surrounding hills. It was still quite cool, and Patrick was wearing a sleeveless sweater as well as his slacks. He advised Andrew to do the same, particularly as they were going to have a two hour drive down the hill to Kandy in an open M.G.

They settled themselves in the car and Andrew revved up the engine so that Patrick could hear all the exciting noises an M.G. makes. Patrick fell in love with the car as quickly as Andrew had done when he first saw it in Nuwara Eliya.

The two young men arrived at Patrick's home just before lunch and started a gentle up-hill climb to the house. Soon after they entered the drive Patrick pointed to some large stable-like sheds. To Andrew's delight he saw the trunks and heads of two elephants inside. He stopped the car and Patrick explained that they were two pet elephants the family had kept since they were babies many years ago. 'One is called Tikkiri and the other Rita. I've known them since I was a baby and they know me too. They had a mother who was devoted to my grandfather. He could do anything with her until, one day, there was a terrible accident and she had to be destroyed.'

'What happened?' asked Andrew.

Patrick looked at his watch. 'Turn off the engine,' he said. 'We have five minutes to spare, so I'll tell you the awful story now.' He went on: 'When we get to the house you will see a large lawn and some white marble steps that lead up to a wide verandah and our drawing room. One day our grandparents were entertaining some visitors from England and, after lunch, my grandfather told one of the servants to bring him a small bunch of bananas and to send for his favourite elephant. The party gathered at the top of the marble steps and the mahout made the elephant kneel and salaam the visitors. She had seen my grandfather, and the bananas – one of her special treats – and so she was delighted to do this. My grandfather held up the bananas and the elephant came forward to the steps. Still holding the bananas, my grandfather slipped on the top step and fell headlong down to the elephant's feet. She was startled and, instinctively, she thought my grandfather was going to attack her. Instinctively again, and to everyone's horror and disbelief, she picked up my grandfather in her trunk and beat him to death on the steps. My poor grandmother took many weeks to recover from the shock and, of course, the elephant was destroyed.'

Andrew looked at Patrick in shock, and was about to say something, but realised that no words could convey his horror at the story. He started the engine, and they drove on in silence until the house came into view. It stood in magnificent gardens and Andrew saw the marble steps at once. He stopped the car under the porch and servants came forward to take their luggage. Two black retrievers came rushing up to Patrick to greet him, and these were followed by his mother. She looked most elegant in a silk sari with her jet-black hair tied in a small bun at the back. Her feet were in gold sandals, which showed off her red toenails, and she hugged Patrick before she turned to Andrew.

'Mr Harvey, Patrick told me that you were tall, but I never expected such a young giant. You see, we Singhalese are small people, usually, and so it comes as a surprise, a very nice surprise, to see such a huge young man. Welcome to Akurana.' She held out her hand which Andrew took.

'Well, thank you, and will you please call me Andrew?'

Mrs Coswatte inclined her head. 'Now Patrick, I'm sure Andrew would like to freshen up after the journey before we have a drink before lunch.'

When Andrew reappeared, Patrick's father had arrived. He was of darker skin than his wife, and a middle-aged spread was just beginning to make itself evident. He was very good-looking and his dignity and handsomeness clearly came from his Kandyan king ancestry.

Mrs Coswatte introduced them and said, 'Mr Harvey would like us to call him Andrew.'

A servant brought round a tray of drinks. Some glasses had a milky white liquid in them, and some pale green. 'Andrew, the green liquid is fresh lime juice, and the white is milk from our young King coconuts; we call them Karumbas. Do try one and we'll have some beer with our lunch.' Andrew did and he found the drink delightful.

'A word about the coconut,' said Patrick's father. 'As you have already seen, we are not short of coconut trees in this island and these are wonderful things, because every part of them has a use. A lot of visitors to our shores think we drink the coconut milk and throw away everything else' This is by no means so. Let me explain.'

'Try and stop him,' said Patrick, putting his arm through his father's.

'Please do tell me about the coconut,' said Andrew.

'Take your drink, for a start,' said Andrew's host. 'The milk comes from a young coconut, and the younger the better. Coconut milk can also become an extremely alcoholic drink. The most popular and cheapest one is toddy. The milk you're drinking is allowed to ferment and is drunk by estate labourers and other workers. Then sometimes the toddy is distilled and I think it turns into a pale golden liquid called arrack. It looks rather like whisky and it can be very potent. The white flesh of the coconut, still with its brown skin, is turned into copra which provides coconut oil, desiccated coconut and so on. The leaves of the tree are plaited and make very good roofing for villagers' huts. The hard shell of the coconut is cut in half and, after the flesh for copra is removed, it is used on rubber estates to catch the latex from the rubber trees and, lastly, the outside husk of the coconut is turned into coir to make mats, ropes and so on. So you see, Andrew, a coconut palm is a godsend to the people of Ceylon.'

'Thank you very much, sir,' said Andrew. 'That was fascinating. I simply had no idea how useful coconut palms are. When I next write to my parents in England I'll tell them all about it. They'll think I'm very clever!'

'Do you only write to your parents, Andrew? Isn't there someone else, a young girl perhaps, that you write to?' asked Mrs Coswatte with a smile and raised eyebrows.

'Yes there is. A young girl I met on the ship coming to Ceylon. We're very much in love and, one day, we hope to marry. Unfortunately the Tea Company I work for won't allow marriage for five years – that's the length of my first agreement.'

'That's very sad, Andrew. Does this mean you won't see your young lady for five years? It's a very long time.'

'It's funny you should ask that, because Mrs Sanders, my P.D.'s wife, has very kindly asked Sarah – my girlfriend – to spend a few weeks with them on Strathmore. People have been so good to me since I've been here – Mr Coswatte and yourself, for instance. It's a wonderful chance for me to see the Pera Hera in such comfort.'

Lunch was announced and the party moved into the dining room. 'I hope you like curry, Andrew,' said Mr Coswatte. 'We are starting you off with a dish called chicken pilau. It consists of a roasted chicken on a bed of savoury yellow rice which is stuffed with fried onions, pieces of hard-boiled egg and raisins. A gently curried sauce comes with the dish and you can pour as much as you want on to your pilau.'

'I'm sure I shall love it,' said Andrew. He spoke the truth because he had a second helping and washed it down with a tankard of Nuwara Eliya beer.

When the dessert arrived, Mr Coswatte spoke. 'I've just given you a lecture on the coconut, Andrew, and now this pudding deserves some explanation. We Singhalese can claim no credit for it because it was introduced to us by the Dutch who invaded and occupied our island two or three hundred years ago. The pudding consists of sago, which has been boiled in coconut milk and flavoured gently with spices. It is then kept in our ice-box. You will see that it is served with two separate sauces. One is coconut milk, and the other is another product of the palm tree, called jaggery. Apart from the mixture being very tasty, it acts as a marvellous digestive. The Dutch were hearty eaters we believe, and after a large lunch, this pudding ensured they had a good sleep until tea time.'

After heartily thanking Patrick's parents for a delicious meal, Andrew was taken by Patrick and shown around the garden, and later, after tea, they left for Kandy, which was a twenty minutes' drive. On the way, Patrick told Andrew that he had two bottles of water and two towels in the car. Looking puzzled, Andrew asked why.

'You'll see quite soon,' said Patrick.

Eventually, they arrived at Kandy, and Patrick directed Andrew to some large sheds not far from the sacred Temple of the Tooth. Patrick explained that, because he had an elder brother and some elderly relations in the main procession, he had special permission to watch the elephants being decorated for the procession. They parked the car and Patrick told Andrew to take off his shoes and socks, and he proceeded to do the same.

Patrick said, 'We're now going to see some thirty or forty elephants being dressed in their rich silks and golds for the Pera Hera, and we're specially privileged to be allowed to watch.'

As the two young men approached the elephant sheds, Andrew's nose told him that he was about to see a lot of elephants. As they entered the main shed he saw the floor was covered with elephant dung. There was a carpet of dung, inches thick, and Andrew realised at once why he had bare feet. Had he been wearing shoes and socks they would have had to be thrown away afterwards.

It was a marvellous and novel sight for Andrew to see so many elephants. Their caparisonings were rich and rare, and the beasts were not exactly enjoying everything that was being done to them. Andrew was lost in amazement at all he saw.

Once they got back to the M.G. Patrick produced the bottles of water and they washed and dried their feet. Then they moved on to the road and stood facing the sacred temple with their backs to the Kandy Lake. They had a little while to wait, but soon enough they head tom-toms in the distance and explosions from firecrackers. Then they heard the sound of horns and, eventually, the leading elephant came into sight preceded by Kandyan dignitaries dressed in white, scarlet and gold. The torches held by others in the procession threw enough light to make the scene almost as bright as day. On either side of the elephants were Kandyan dancers and, here again, they were lavishly dressed in white sarongs, tucked up to below their knees with much gold jewellery round their necks and over their bare chests. The procession took a long time to pass, and the leading elephant, carrying the casket containing the sacred tooth relic, followed by many other elephants, finally disappeared from sight.

Patrick and Andrew drove back to the Coswatte's *walauwa* or home – and sat down to a late supper.

The next morning after breakfast – a meal of egg hoppers and coffee – they moved into the garden at Mrs Coswatte's suggestion.

'Did you enjoy your egg hoppers, Andrew?' Mrs Coswatte asked.

'I loved them,' he replied, 'and I would love to know what they're made of. I've never even seen one before.'

'We make a thin batter of flour and water and then, very carefully, we break an egg and pour it into the middle of the batter. We then fry the hopper, and that's what you had for your breakfast.' She paused and put a hand on Andrew's shoulder. She pointed: 'Look, Andrew, here comes our pet elephant for her morning drink of water.'

Andrew turned and saw an elephant plodding up the drive being led by her mahout. 'Just watch,' said Mrs Coswatte.

Andrew watched and saw the mahout release his hold on the elephant's rope. She walked a few more paces towards them, stopped, and turned towards a tap near some croton bushes. She turned the tap with her trunk and had a long drink. When she had finished she turned the tap off again. Andrew watched with amazement and delight as she turned towards them and raised her trunk as a sort of 'thank you'.

'That's her morning trick,' said Patrick. 'Would you like a ride?'

'I'd love one,' said Andrew and, with the mahout's help, he clambered on to the elephant's knee and from there to her neck. The mahout led them away and they returned about a quarter of an hour later.

When Andrew had dismounted, Patrick asked, 'How are you?'

'Sore,' said Andrew. 'I shouldn't have been wearing shorts. That elephant's neck is like a hedgehog's back!'

After lunch Andrew thanked the Coswattes for their kindness and he and Patrick drove back to Strathmore.

Chapter 8

The first thing Andrew did after seeing Patrick off was to rush into his bungalow to see if there was any response from Sarah to the Sanders' invitation to visit Strathmore. There was none and Andrew realised that, although Sarah would undoubtedly telegraph her reply, his invitation letter to her would still take some days to reach her.

Whilst Andrew was away in Kandy for the Pera Hera, Angela Sanders was doing some serious thinking, and the idea that was forming in her head would not go away.

She and Peter were strolling in the garden on the Sunday evening of Andrew's return and the sun was setting on the far western horizon. They had glasses of whisky in their hands. Angela put her arm through Peter's and led him towards a stone bench where they sat down. Peter looked at her in a puzzled way.

'I've been worried about Andrew,' Angela began, 'but before I say any more, tell me this. Are you happy with his work? Do you think he is happy here? Do you think he wants to make tea planting a career for life?'

'What are you up to, you scheming woman? I know these are not idle questions. You're up to something, aren't you?'

'You answer my questions first, and then I'll tell you what I'm up to, said Angela.

Peter put his hand over his wife's. 'Yes, I'm very pleased with Andrew. I'm sure he wants to devote his life to tea planting. I say this because, if you remember, I put Andrew in charge when we started taking in Nankawella's green leaf after their factory caught fire. Andrew is still handling this extra work very well, and he still has some months to go. I'd hate to lose Andrew. Now, what's on your mind?'

'Well, it's this,' said Angela. 'Andrew has had a very rough time since he's been on Strathmore. First he had the homosexual drama with Mark Howell in his bath, then the missing cooly pay business, then the district rumours about him being a homosexual. In spite of

94

all this you say he works very well. So I think he deserves some encouragement, some sort of reward.'

'I think I know what you're going to say, but spell it out for me,' said the P.D.

'I think the reason why Andrew has worked so well under such trying circumstances is because of his love for his girlfriend, Sarah. You saw the way in which his face lit up when we said he could invite her to Strathmore for a few weeks. Now I know full well Andrew is on his first agreement, so I know he cannot marry for five years. I know all that. But I also know that you are a substantial shareholder in the Latimer Tea Company, and finally I know that my brother, your brother-in-law, is a director of the Latimer Tea Company. Write and ask them for special permission for Andrew to marry now if he wants to. Say you know it's creating a precedent, but emphasize you consider this is a very special case which should be considered on compassionate grounds. I really think you should.'

'You *have* been a busy little bee, haven't you, Mrs Sanders?'

'Peter, I said at the start that I've been doing some serious thinking. There's something about Andrew, something exceptional, that's worth encouraging, worth saving.'

Peter Sanders paused and stared at a bush of anthurium lilies to his right. He turned to his wife. 'This takes some digesting, but I'll say this. I like your idea. For the moment I can't think of any objections. Let me sleep on it and we'll talk it over at breakfast in the morning.'

Peter Sanders came straight to the point at breakfast. 'Yes, I think it's important to give Andrew someone who is on his side, a wife, some form of stabilizing assurance. I think he's well worth treating as a special, compassionate case. So I'll do what you suggest. I'll write to London today. I should do this through our Colombo Agents, but I'll ring Derek Scott this morning and tell him what I'm doing.'

'You are a darling,' said Angela and walked round the table and kissed her husband.

Peter Sanders was as good as his word and, after a telephone conversation with the senior partner in his Colombo Agents' office, he wrote to London putting up a good case for Andrew being allowed to marry early on compassionate grounds.

On the Monday Andrew found a letter from Sarah in the tappal bag. He didn't get too excited because he knew it must have been written before she received her invitation to visit Strathmore. Having read the letter Andrew felt that Mrs Sanders must have second sight or clairvoyant tendencies. Sarah was missing her ship-board friend a great deal. She said more than once in her letter that she was desperately in love with Andrew, that she couldn't possibly wait for five years and so, she said, she had had an idea. Sarah said that she had spoken to her father and explained to him that waiting for five years to marry Andrew would kill her. Her father told her that both he and her mother had been watching her anxiously lately and they were both well aware of her predicament.

Sarah then dropped the bombshell. She said her father was more than ready to give Andrew a job in England if he was prepared to abandon his planting career. She said that her father had gone further than this. He had said that Andrew would get a salary that would be more than enough to keep Sarah and himself in comfort for the rest of their lives. In the remainder of her letter Sarah pleaded with Andrew to accept her father's offer and to come back to England and marry her as soon as he could.

Andrew put the letter down and walked outside to his small lawn. He sat on the grass and gave himself time to think. It didn't take too long for him to come to a conclusion. He decided that he would do nothing until he had Sarah's reaction to the Sanders' invitation for her to visit Strathmore. He then found himself thinking as to whether he wanted to leave tea planting and work in England.

He came back to the point that he must discuss things with Sarah. He hoped that by now she had had his letter and the invitation, which, indeed, she had, and that evening the estate clerk rang Andrew in his bungalow and said that a telegram was waiting for him in the estate office. Andrew was in the M.G. in a flash and ten minutes later the telegram was in his hand. It read:

Ecstatic – sailing tomorrow. Arriving Colombo Harbour crack of dawn on fourteenth. Please thank Sanders for wonderful invitation. All my love. Sarah.'

Andrew almost wept with relief. He drove from the estate office to the P.D.'s bungalow. Mrs Sanders was dead-heading some roses and Peter Sanders was watching her from a garden bench. She looked up when she heard the M.G. and saw the car stop under the porch. Andrew got out of the car and ran towards her. Peter Sanders had joined his wife as Andrew arrived, and Andrew thrust the telegram into her hand.

'We seem to have done the right thing, Andy,' said Angela Sanders, handing the telegram to her husband. 'I'm so glad for you.'

'Sarah asks me to thank you for your generous invitation,' said Andrew. 'Well, I do with all my heart, and I can't thank you enough. I say this because I also had a letter from Sarah yesterday. She sounded very depressed and said she dreaded the next five years waiting to marry me. She had written, of course, before she had had my letter with your wonderful invitation. And now we have the telegram. It speaks for itself, I think.'

Angela Sanders put her arm round Andrew and kissed him. 'I'm so very, very glad, Andy.'

'Here, watch it!' said Peter Sanders, pretending to be cross. 'You're married to me, you know, not my S.D. Only joking,' he added. 'Let's sit down and discuss matters.'

They moved to the verandah. 'I'll give you two days leave, Andrew, the thirteenth and fourteenth. Muttusamy will take you down to Colombo in the Buick on the thirteenth and you can arrange to stay somewhere that night. I'll call our Colombo Agents and ask them to get you a pass to go on board Sarah's ship and, in all probability, they'll let you have the office launch to meet Sarah and bring her ashore. Muttusamy will then drive you both back to Strathmore. How's that?'

'Very generous, sir. Mrs Sanders and you have been so kind to me since I first arrived on Strathmore. I don't know how I shall ever be able to repay you.'

Naturally Andrew said nothing about the offer of a job in England. He felt quite sure he could persuade Sarah to wait something over four years until they could marry. His confidence was based on the likelihood that somehow Sarah would visit him every year. After all, her father was chairman of a major steamship company and if *he* couldn't give his daughter a free return passage to Ceylon every year, it would be a pretty poor show!

Andrew's happiness and gratefulness would have been ten times greater had he known that the Sanders were trying to get permission for him to marry Sarah without waiting for five years.

After a start to his planting career which had had some unpleasant moments, it seemed to him that that was now all over and done with and that he had nothing but happiness now to look forward to.

With the time difference between Ceylon and England being approximately five hours, Andrew realised he could send a telegram to Sarah before she sailed. The estate clerk Chidambaram was still at his desk and, with his help, Andrew telephoned the post office and dictated a telegram that would make a certain young lady in England very happy indeed.

Andrew saw his P.D. the next morning in the factory, and told him again how very touched and grateful he was to them both for their wonderful invitation to Sarah.

'Well, Andrew,' said the P.D., 'my wife and I have been feeling very sorry for you. You've had a rough time on Strathmore since you've been here. And, in spite of the things that have happened to you, you've still done your work without flinching. I'm very pleased with your work. The labour force likes you. Murugiah tells me you've tried very hard with your Tamil – you're getting quite fluent, he says. So, with one thing and another, we both felt we would like to give you a little present. A present soon on her way to you by sea – Sarah.'

Andrew was very moved. He just nodded his thanks to the P.D. and turned away quickly in embarrassment. He felt that the next week or so would pass very slowly until Sarah arrived, particularly so because there could be no communication between them until they met on the fourteenth.

However, he had underestimated Sarah's ingenuity. She was not the daughter of a large steamship company chairman for nothing. At each port at which they called, the Agent came aboard early in the morning. Sarah made much of each gentleman with the result that, on returning to his office ashore, he sent a telegram composed by Sarah to Andrew. There were four such telegrams and they did much to help Andrew in his impatience to see his adored Sarah in Colombo harbour.

The day before Sarah's arrival finally dawned and, as Andrew was finishing his breakfast, he saw the Buick arrive with a grinning Muttusamy at the wheel. They had an uneventful drive down to Colombo, and Muttusamy drove straight to Martin Phillips' bungalow where he had spent his first night in Ceylon. This was a good move because, when Andrew had telephoned Martin, a week earlier, he knew he would be going to Sarah's ship early in the morning in his office launch, and Andrew cadged a lift.

Andrew went to bed early, and he and Martin were alongside the vast white hulk of the vessel soon after she had anchored. They were the first up the gangway and, near the top, Andrew saw Sarah waiting and his heart leaped. She rushed towards him and they embraced fiercely. A tactful Martin Phillips went along to the Purser's office.

After a few moments, Sarah took Andrew's hand and led the way to her cabin. She had already packed and they hugged each other again. 'Why are you crying?' asked Andrew. 'Are you disappointed to see me?' he said in a jokingly serious voice.

'You idiot,' said Sarah, wiping away her tears with a little hankie. 'It's because I'm delighted and overjoyed to see you. Oh, Andy, I've so longed and longed for this moment. I've felt so desperate at times dreading the five years I thought we would have to wait before seeing each other again. I will never be able to thank the Sanders enough for their very kind invitation.' They hugged each other again and Sarah kissed Andrew passionately.

They were interrupted by a knock on the cabin door and Martin Phillips' wharf clerk stood outside with a crew member from the launch. Between them they gathered up Sarah's luggage and took it to the launch. Muttusamy was waiting on the passenger jetty with a baggage cooly and they departed with Sarah's bags to the Buick.

After introducing Sarah to Muttusamy, he said to Sarah, 'Would you like to sit in front, darling? You'll get a better view of the road to Kandy.'

'Not a hope,' she replied. 'I'm sitting in the back with you. Anyway, I've been to Kandy before and I can't make a pass at you if I'm in the front and you're in the back!'

Muttusamy pointed out the usual sights on the way to Kandy and, in a little over two hours, he stopped the Buick in front of the Queens Hotel. After a fairly light lunch they started off up the Ramboda Pass to Strathmore. Before they arrived Sarah asked Andrew what the Sanders were like.

'They're simply charming,' said Andrew. 'You'll feel at home at once. They're very easy-going.'

'How did this invitation to me to stay come about? I hope, darling, you didn't hint that there was nothing I'd adore more.'

'No, I'll tell you the truth. You know from my letters that I've had one or two unpleasant moments since I arrived on Strathmore – the trouble with Mark Howell, the missing cooly pay, and so on.' Sarah nodded. 'Well.' Andrew continued, 'the Sanders felt that I'd come through the dramas pretty well and they knew I was in love with you and that I was missing you terribly. Peter Sanders told me one morning that he was very pleased with my work and that he and his wife felt a visit from you would go some way to make up for the bad times. That's the whole, unvarnished, truth.'

Muttusamy turned off the main road on to the cart road to

99

Strathmore. Andrew recalled the first time he had done this so many months ago.

They drew up in front of the P.D.'s bungalow and, as before, Stock and Trigger, the golden retrievers, came bounding out to greet them. By the time the young couple had left the car, Angela Sanders had appeared on the verandah. Sarah went straight to her and embraced her, somewhat to her hostess' surprise.

'I had to do that, Mrs Sanders – I simply did it instinctively. I've been thinking about you so much since I received your wonderful invitation to visit you. You really are the kindest person in the world, and I shall never be able to thank you enough.'

By this time, the P.D.'s lady had recovered her composure. 'You mustn't feel indebted, Sarah, my dear. As you say, you hugged me instinctively and I loved it! That little gesture is, in itself, a very big "thank you" and we are delighted to have you.' She turned to Andrew. 'Andrew, I'll take care of Sarah now and we shall expect you for dinner this evening. Muttusamy will drop you back at your bungalow. Come along at about seven-thirty.'

'Thank you, Mrs Sanders. I shall look forward to it. Bye, Sarah, my love. I'll see you this evening. I can't wait.'

As Andrew was getting into the Buick, he caught a glimpse of Mrs Sanders leading Sarah away, an arm around her young guest's shoulder.

Andrew glanced at Muttusamy as they drove down to his bungalow. Muttusamy was grinning hugely. 'And what are you grinning about, Muttusamy?' Andrew asked.

'Your young missy lady very pretty girl, no? I think master will soon marry her and I will be asked to wedding, no?'

'You're an old rogue, Muttusamy, but I hope you will chauffeur us at our wedding. You're wrong about marrying soon, though. I can't marry until I've spent another four years here in Ceylon.'

'That is hopeless, no? Why you can't marry for more than four years?'

'Because the company does not allow young creepers and young S.D.'s to marry for the first five years in the job.'

'Then, sir, you must arrange for your missy to stay until you can marry. I will pray at my temple for this to happen.'

'Thank you, Muttusamy,' said Andrew, and patted the driver's shoulder.

In the evening Andrew drove up to the P.D.'s bungalow and Sarah rose from a cane chair on the verandah and came to meet him. She looked as fresh as a daisy, in a flowered cotton frock with a pale lemon cardigan over her shoulders. 'So this is the famous M.G., Andy. What a beauty.' She came down the steps as Andrew was getting out of the car and they embraced. 'I'm longing for a drive in her.'

'Tomorrow, I hope, my darling,' said Andrew as the P.D. appeared.

After greeting Andrew, the P.D. and his guests moved into the drawing room where a wood fire was blazing. 'That's a sight I didn't expect to see,' said Sarah. She moved over to it and warmed her hands.

'Yes,' said Peter Sanders. 'You see, we're nearly six thousand feet high up here and it gets chilly at nights. Why, near Nuwara Eliya they get frosts at night at certain times of the year.'

Mrs Sanders appeared, followed by their head boy who moved to the drinks table and looked round expectantly. The P.D. nodded to him and a cork popped.

'Sarah, we don't have champagne every day,' explained Mrs Sanders, 'but we feel that this is rather a special occasion: to welcome you to Strathmore.' She paused. 'And for another reason,' she added, and looked towards her husband.

When their glasses were in their hands Peter Sanders turned to Sarah. 'Welcome to Strathmore, my dear,' he said. 'We are genuinely glad to have you here and we hope you will be very happy.' They drank.

'Now, as my wife has just said, there's another reason for the champagne. We may be quite wrong,' he said with a cheeky grin on his face, 'but we get the impression that you and Andrew are quite fond of each other.' Andrew took Sarah's hand in his and the P.D. went on. 'Sarah, Andrew has had a pretty rough time since he's been on Strathmore, so Angela and I thought we should cheer him up a bit by inviting you here.'

Sarah blushed delightfully and murmured, 'Thank you very much indeed.'

'But we've gone a bit further than that,' said the P.D.

Andrew looked a little puzzled, and Sarah's hand tightened in his.

'After Angela had decided to have you to stay, we did a lot more thinking. We felt strongly that, whilst a few weeks' visit from Sarah was all very well in its own way, it was, somehow, not enough. So I chanced my arm.'

Sarah and Andrew were now *really* puzzled.

The P.D. went on. 'I wrote to the Latimer board in London. I told them in full what had been going on here. I told them that I thought that you, Andrew, had all the makings of a first class tea planter and that I didn't want to lose you. I said that I felt there was a chance that I might lose you, because you were seriously in love with a young lady in England. I said that I was pretty sure that if you were in England too, both of you would marry without hesitation. Finally, I said that I thought if you had to wait in excess of four years before you could marry, it was distinctly possible that I might lose you and, I went on in the letter, that I should leave the remedy to the discretion of the directors. Shall I go on?'

Neither Sarah nor Andrew could speak. They just nodded and Mrs Sanders had her handkerchief to her mouth to hide her laughter.

'Well, to cut a long letter short, the official position is that, if you want to, you can marry as soon as you like and, of course, your pay goes up to a married S.D.'s level.'

Sarah burst into tears.

'My dear,' said the P.D. in mock alarm holding her arm, 'I thought you *wanted* to marry the wretched boy!'

'I do, I do' sobbed Sarah. 'I'm so happy.' She threw her arms round Peter Sanders and kissed him soundly. She then turned to Andrew and repeated the performance. Finally she hugged Angela Sanders.

When some order had been restored and glasses re-charged, Andrew led Sarah to a chair and made her sit down. He turned to his host and hostess. 'I know this is normally done privately,' he said, 'but I can't wait.' He knelt at Sarah's feet. 'My lovely darling, will you please marry me?'

'I think I'm dreaming,' said Sarah, 'but, in case I'm not, I'd love to marry you, Andy, my darling.'

Angela's laughter turned to tears. 'I'm such a sentimental fool,' she said, 'but that was the most moving little scene. We must have a lot more champagne! I'll see if there's another bottle on ice.' She left the room but was back again a few moments later. She went up to Sarah. 'Many, many years ago, Sarah, a dear Aunt did a sweet thing. Peter had just proposed to me in Edinburgh and he told my Aunt what had happened. She disappeared and came back with a small box. She opened it and inside was a lovely sapphire and diamond ring. She told me it was her engagement ring and she wanted Peter to put it on my finger at once and that I was to wear it until Peter had given me my own ring. Now I'm going to do exactly the same thing.' She held out her palm to Sarah and in it lay an emerald and diamond ring. 'This is my engagement ring Sarah. Please wear it until Andrew gives you your own.'

It was Sarah's turn to shed a tear.

Dinner was a very happy occasion, with the champagne having its usual effect. The party moved out to the verandah, intending to have coffee there, but they found it was too chilly. They paused for just a few moments to admire a glorious full moon, seemingly almost within touching distance.

'What is that noise?' asked Sarah.

'Actually, it's two noises,' said Peter Sanders. 'The closer noise is cicadas, a sort of grasshopper, and I believe they make the noise you hear by rubbing their back legs together. It must be true because everyone will give you this reason. The other noise comes from frogs. We have masses of them, and they come out at night for their starlight serenade.' They all laughed, and they moved into the drawing room where it was warmer for coffee.

'Andy,' said Angela, 'I'd like to tell you something, and I think what I'm going to say will possibly explain some things which may have puzzled you. I think you know that Peter and I have no children. Well, I'm not a particularly impressionable type of woman, but since the day you arrived on Strathmore I've been seeing a lot of you. We've had many chats and I feel I know you quite well. I watched you come through all your difficulties here, and I admired your courage in the way you handled them. I've thought about you a lot, and I've grown to love you – yes, love you.' Seeing the startled look on both Andrew's and Sarah's faces, she hastily continued: 'Don't be alarmed, both of you. My love for Andy is purely maternal, I promise you, and Peter knows all about it.' She put a hand on Andrew's arm. 'In a nutshell,Andy, I wish you were my son. There, now I've said it.'

There was a heavy silence, and Andrew walked over to his hostess, put his hands on her shoulders and kissed the top of her head. 'You do me a great honour. I'm so touched,' he said softly, 'so very, very touched.' He walked over to the french doors leading on to the verandah and stood looking into the garden. He came back. 'I don't know what to say, Mrs Sanders. All I know is that I feel so – so honoured. I can think of no other word to describe it.'

Peter Sanders thought it was time to bring the party down to earth again. 'Andrew, tomorrow is Saturday and so you and Sarah have the weekend to yourselves. There will be a great deal you will want to discuss now that you know that you can marry whenever you want to. The first thing is, of course, that you will want to give your parents the good news and you should telegraph them first thing in the morning. However, when it comes to dates, and where and when you will marry, and in fact anything to do with Strathmore and your duties here, you will need to bring Angela and me into the discussion. After all' – he gave his wife a quick glance – 'as it seems we are now almost your foster parents, please keep us posted on developments.' Angela threw a table mat at him.

'Of course we will, sir. I'd like to start by driving Sarah round Strathmore in the morning, and we can discuss our plans as we go along. Of course we shall keep you fully in the picture all the time. I'm sure I speak for Sarah when I say what a sense of relief we have when we know we have you and Mrs Sanders to come to when we're unsure about something.'

After they all had finished their coffee, Andrew bade everyone goodnight, saying that he would pick Sarah up the following morning for her tour around Strathmore.

Andrew collected Sarah in the M.G. just after breakfast as promised, and Mrs Sanders had lent her an old topee of hers as Andrew had the hood of the car down. Sarah walked slowly round the car, admiring it. 'I've got an international driving licence, darling, but don't worry – I shan't ask you to let me drive her until I know more about road conditions up country. Now what do we do this morning?'

'Well, first we drive to Nuwara Eliya and send off our telegrams. Then we'll have lunch at the Grand Hotel, and this afternoon I'll show you round Strathmore. How's that?'

'Lovely,' said Sarah. 'How far is Nuwara Eliya?'

'About an hour's drive and about a thousand feet higher than we are now, so let's be off!'

They drove to the Post Office and composed their telegrams. They read them out to each other and then handed them to the Tamil clerk behind the counter. He read them through and looked up shyly. 'Can I wish you good luck, sir? I am very happy for you and your young lady. I hope you will be very happy.'

Sarah blushed, but managed to say, 'Thank you,' in an embarrassed voice.

The couple drove to the Grand Hotel and sat on the front lawn. They ordered drinks and, for the first time since Sarah's arrival in Ceylon, they had an uninterrupted hour or so to themselves.

Andrew started the ball rolling. 'I've always been told that a wedding day is the "bride's day", and so, over to you, my darling. Tell me what you would like to do.'

'Andy, darling, that question is going to take some answering, so sit back and enjoy your beer and listen to your future wife!' She sipped her Pimms. 'First, these are just my ideas and please, please, they are open to discussion, because to me it is so important that we are both happy with the final arrangements on which we agree. Now, you may think this strange, but I would like to marry you in Ceylon. You see, if I chose England, it would mean you would have to ask for at least two months' leave. I think the Sanders have been simply wonderful in getting permission for you to marry me now. Then they have been so kind in letting me stay in their bungalow. And, finally, you now know what Mrs Sanders thinks of you. For all these reasons I'd like to become Mrs Harvey in Ceylon.'

'You've taken a ton weight off my mind, darling. I kept on waking up last night wondering how on earth I could get enough leave to marry you in England. Bless you. Ceylon it shall be, but the wedding should be in Colombo, not Strathmore or Nuwara Eliya, for reasons of accommodation, transport and so on.'

'Ah! I hadn't thought of that, but of course: it must be Colombo. Have you any further thoughts than just Colombo for the wedding?'

'Yes, I have, quite a lot. But, as you have just said, they're open to negotiation. Not just you and me but our parents as well. We'll write and tell them what we would like and then it's really your father and mother who make the final decisions.'

'Tell me, O wise one, what ideas do you have?'

'Darling, I said I was awake a lot last night. Well, I did a lot of thinking then, all on the lines of a Colombo wedding. I happened to remember that when Martin Phillips, the young man from our Colombo Agents who met me on the ship when I first arrived, was driving me back to his bungalow he pointed out various buildings. First he pointed out the Galle Face Hotel. He said it was used for all sorts of parties and things. He mentioned wedding receptions and he said the hotel was particularly popular for these because there were two churches within half a mile radius. One was a Scots Kirk and the other a C of E church. Then I remembered that before Martin drove me to his house we walked through the Fort. The Fort is the main business and shopping centre of Colombo and there are tailors galore. I had shorts and shirts and things made, and I know ladies have dresses made there. There are jewellers too. So that takes care of most things and the details can be worked out later. As for our honeymoon, this is solely and exclusively my affair. I mean the planning only. I very much want you to be with me on the honeymoon itself. Only joking!'

'You'd better be "only joking", my darling – you try and stop me, Buster!'

They discussed plans through lunch and throughout the afternoon. Sarah tried to concentrate whilst they were driving around Strathmore and, although she took in a lot of what Andrew was saying about tea cultivation and manufacture. her thoughts kept wandering back to the sudden and wonderful way in which both her's and Andrew's lives had changed overnight. She was still dreaming when she realised that the M.G. had stopped and Andrew was getting out. He was saying, 'This is our hospital, and we have our own doctor.' She pulled herself together.

They walked up the steps on to the verandah of the hospital and into the one and only ward. Sarah was happily surprised to see pink and blue covers on some cots at one end of the ward. 'That's where our newborn babies are kept,' began Andrew, and then he stopped and turned to Sarah. 'And this is our own medico, Doctor Coomasaru.'

After introducing Sarah, the doctor shook Sarah's hand warmly and said, 'May I show you round? There's not an awful lot to see, but I'm becoming quite proud of this little hospital and, although I'm relatively new, I'm enjoying doing what I can to keep my patients happy.'

The visit didn't take long and the young couple were soon in the M.G. again making for Andrew's bungalow for tea.

They hadn't been driving for more than a few moments when Sarah put her hand on Andrew's arm. 'Stop for a moment, Andy, will you? I've just thought of something.'

Andrew stopped the car and turned to Sarah enquiringly. 'What is it, darling?' he asked.

'Andy, we've just telegraphed our parents telling them we're engaged, but we've told them nothing else. I think we should follow up this morning's telegrams saying we want to get married in Colombo. Then we ask them to get together at their end and tell us what sort of date would suit them for our wedding. What do you think?'

'I think that not only are you very beautiful and sexy but that you also have a brain!'

Sarah leant across and bit his ear. 'How do we go about these extra telegrams, darling?' she asked.

'We race straight back to Nuwara Eliya and send them off from the Post Office, if it's still open. Can you think of suitable wordings as we go along?'

Within the hour two more telegrams were on their way to England and Andrew and Sarah were on their way back to Strathmore.

The telegrams were despatched on the Saturday and on the following Wednesday evening, both Sarah and Andrew had their replies. These were comprehensive, but similar in content, and were to the effect that both families had spoken to each other on the telephone and that Sarah's father had booked passages on one of his ships for the four parents, arriving in Colombo in three weeks time. Sarah's parents' telegram added that they needed to know urgently the date of the wedding so that invitations could be drafted. They made it clear that the wedding date should be fixed by Andrew with his employers, as he was the only one who had to ask for permission. Finally they assured Andrew that, of course, all the wedding expenses were on the Allenby account and there was no need for him to worry on that score.

Lady Allenby turned to her husband. 'Colin, it seems to me that we are going to see a lot of the Harvey family in the next few weeks. Don't you think we should meet before we catch the ship?'

'I've been thinking exactly the same thing,' said Sir Colin. 'Shall we make it the Club, or shall we invite them to dinner at a restaurant?'

'Oh, I think the Club. It will be far quieter than a restaurant. We'll be able to chat more easily. Shall I ring the Harveys?'

'Yes, do it now. We haven't got an awful lot of time before we sail.'

What was intended to be a fairly short telephone call turned out to be a lengthy affair between the two ladies. In the end it was agreed that the families would meet for dinner at Sir Colin's club the next evening. Anthea Harvey asked whether she might bring her daughter Pamela with them because they would like to take her on the ship to Colombo as well. Lady Allenby was delighted.

The two families met and settled themselves down to drinks before dinner. There was no question of shyness or the need for ice to be broken. They found themselves happily interrupting each other and they felt they were already old friends before they moved into dinner. Both ladies felt an acute sense of relief that they had got on so well. They all seemed to think alike, and there were hardly any areas of disagreement on any of the points they discussed.

The only exception was when William Harvey made it clear that the cost of Pamela's passage and their own passages was to be met by himself. Colin Allenby would have none of it. They were on Christian name terms by now. 'My dear William,' he said, 'have you forgotten

107

that I'm Chairman of the wretched steamship line? My terms include any passages I want and I don't pay for them. When I accepted the appointment I made it clear to my fellow directors that I had no intention of being treated like a dashed stowaway!'

The party broke up just before midnight and they were all agreed that the sailing date couldn't come too soon.

Their wish was granted. Time seemed to fly and in no time at all they found themselves on board a dazzling white liner in Tilbury, preparing to sail for the East. The Captain, on discovering that the Company Chairman and his party were on board, naturally arranged for them all to sit at his table. The Purser, for his part, gave the Harveys rather special accommodation near the Chairman's suite.

The voyage was uneventful so far as the grown-up Allenbys and Harveys were concerned. This was not the case for Pamela Harvey. The young ship's officers found her delectable in the extreme and, whilst after dinner they danced her off her feet, later than that, when most passengers were safely abed, they displayed their ingenuity and intimate knowledge of the ship by taking her to various nooks and crannies where they petted and cuddled safe from prying eyes.

From the beginning of the voyage Sir Colin and his wife found themselves constantly remembering the earlier occasion when they had Andrew Harvey at their table. They found that Andrew had not gone into any great detail with his parents about his experiences with Cynthia Jepson. They told the Harveys just how well Andrew had behaved, how well he had coped with such a frightful and frightening situation, considering how young he was.

Lady Allenby remarked that they had not so far thought about where they were to stay in Colombo after the ship arrived, or how or when they would see their young, or when they would go up country. She said, 'We seem to have left in such a rush we haven't really planned anything.'

Anthea Harvey interrupted. 'I'm so sorry, I should have read out Andrew's telegram to you. In it he said to us that all accommodation, transport and timings were being arranged. I'm sure we'll be put fully in the picture when the two come on board to meet us.'

At the time Anthea Harvey was speaking, all the main arrangements had been made, although some had been only tentatively agreed whilst waiting for the approval of the Allenbys and Harveys. A very full discussion had taken place at the P.D.'s bungalow. The wedding day had been arranged for just three or four weeks after both sets of parents and Pamela had arrived. Peter Sanders had given Andrew and Sarah a resumé of what he, as Andrew's P.D., was prepared to do.

'Andrew,' said Peter Sanders, 'first, I'll deal with your leave. I'm ready to give you three weeks, to be taken in two parts. The first week is for Sarah and you to go to Colombo to meet your parents on the ship. See them safely housed, I suggest, in the Galle Face Hotel, and then spend the rest of the week shopping and making your plans. Our Colombo Agents are giving you their launch and their wharf clerk to help with the baggage from the ship. They will be in contact with the ship's agents to make sure that their arrangements are not going to clash with those of the ship's agents. I mean, the ship's agents know their Chairman is on board, and so they will undoubtedly be planning to send one of their grand launches with a welcoming party to meet Sir Colin. They might do the same about a limousine. Anyway, that will all be sorted out.'

He went on: 'I don't imagine you will all want to spend a whole week in Colombo so, as soon as you know the form, phone us and I will send Muttusamy down in the Buick to bring the Allenbys and your parents and your sister up country. I've spoken to the secretary of the Hill Club in Nuwara Eliya and he will be delighted to make both families temporary members. They will be far more comfortable at the Hill Club than at the Grand Hotel. The second part of your leave, the remaining two weeks, is for your honeymoon and, of course, all those arrangements are for Sarah and you to make!'

Andrew looked at Sarah who seemed a little dewy eyed. She was the first to speak. 'I don't know what to say, Mr Sanders – you are so generous and the thought you have given to all this, and the trouble you have gone to in making such perfect arrangements for Andrew and me are more than I can believe. Thank you both so much. I can't begin to thank you both for all the kindness you have shown me.' She looked at Mrs Sanders. 'You told Andrew the other day that you loved him.' She turned to Peter Sanders, walked up to him, put an arm round his waist and looked up at him. 'What about me? Do I get a look in?'

He grabbed her and gave her a long kiss full on the lips. 'Does that answer your question? And that's only for starters! Of course I love you, Sarah darling, we both do.' He added: 'And, of course, Andrew does too, and so it seems you are much loved by everyone!'

'Well, I love you all too, but especially my darling Andrew. I didn't realise what an all-absorbing, powerful emotion love was until I had known Andrew for a week or two. I am utterly devoted to him. He absorbs me night and day. My love for him cannot die until I do.'

There was a slightly embarrassed silence, which was broken by Peter Sanders. 'I think we should all have a drink.'

Time flew by, and all of a sudden it was only ten days before both sets of parents and Andrew's sister were due in Colombo harbour.

Chapter 9

It was early evening, and Andrew had driven Sarah towards the factory to look at a new shipment of plywood tea-chests that the Teamaker had reported as being not up to standard. The couple were passing through some cooly lines when they saw a small puppy squirming about in the middle of the road and obviously in pain.

'Andy! Stop, stop!' cried Sarah, and she was out of the car in a flash, bending down to pick up the little creature. The puppy's mother, hiding behind a firewood stack, flew at her and buried her teeth in her arm just above the elbow. Some coolies rushed out and drove the dog away, and Andrew then saw it was frothing at the mouth.

'*Piety nai, piety nai,*' the coolies shouted, and Andrew translated for Sarah's benefit.

'They're saying the dog is mad. Into the car, my darling, as quick as you can.' He tied his handkerchief round the wound as tightly as he could to stop the circulation, reversed the car and stormed down the hill.

Sarah had turned quite pale. 'Where are we going?' she asked.

'To the hospital. I hope to goodness the doctor is in. Anyway, even if he's not, the dispenser will be there.'

'Why all the panic, Andy? My arm doesn't need stitching or anything. It was bleeding only a little before you bandaged me up. It'll be OK by the morning. Let's go to your bungalow and have a drink instead.'

'That dog was frothing at the mouth. That could mean it's rabid. The coolies were saying it was mad. We keep rabies injections in the hospital, and you're going to be injected at once, my darling, I'm not taking any chances.'

Luckily, they found the doctor at the hospital, hitting a tennis ball up against a wall of the hospital. He dropped his racket and ran over to the car. 'Trouble?' he asked.

'Miss Allenby has been bitten by a dog in the lines near the factory.

It was frothing at the mouth and the coolies were shouting that it was mad.'

'Follow me, as quickly as you can,' said the doctor, and sprinted inside the hospital.

Soon after Andrew had settled Sarah in a chair, Dr Coomasaru returned with a syringe. 'This is an anti-rabies injection, Miss Allenby. It's rather a large one, I'm afraid, and, even worse, you must have ten or eleven more, one every day. The good news is that you've come to me so quickly that, after the course of injections is over, you'll be as right as rain. You will not develop rabies – that is a terrible thing to contract. I'm quite confident that you will not be infected because we've nipped it in the bud, so to speak. I mean, you having your first injection within minutes of being bitten, and that is the most important thing. You may, though, have a mild reaction to the injection.'

'What would have happened to me had I not seen you so quickly?' asked Sarah.

Dr Coomasaru paused and looked at Sarah steadily. 'Nothing for some weeks, then convulsions and, in four or five days, you would die. But don't even think about these awful possibilities – they're not going to happen. You have my word on it!'

'One more thing, Doc. If it's not too much trouble,' said Andrew, 'will you please get through to the Teamaker and ask him to arrange for someone to go and shoot that dog at once. He'll be there; he's expecting me. Please explain what's happened.'

'Consider it done,' said Coomasaru, and he went on, 'As I've said, Miss Allenby, I must inject you every day for the next eleven days. I'll come to Mrs Sanders' bungalow every morning to do it. Will about nine o'clock be convenient?'

'Perfectly convenient, thank you very much.'

As Andrew was driving her to the big bungalow, Sarah put her arm through his. 'What a charming man, Andy, and what a charming manner. I feel so sure that I couldn't be in better hands.'

'I agree. I've no personal experience of Coomasaru to go on, but I was very impressed too.'

Angela Sanders was most concerned when Andrew told her what had happened, and insisted that Sarah came in at once and rested. 'The shock of the bite was bad enough, but I believe the injections are pretty nasty too, so a little rest before dinner will do you no harm. Andy, come and join us at about half-past seven.'

At dinner that evening the subject of Sarah's dog bite came up more than once. 'There will still be one or two injections for Sarah to have when you both leave for Colombo to meet your parents, Andrew,' said Peter Sanders. 'I'll arrange with our Agents' doctor to give you these, but it will be handy if you go with the remaining injections in your bag. I'll fix this with Coomasaru.'

'What an inconvenient bore this wretched business is,' said Sarah. 'It couldn't have come at a worse time.'

'No, but look on the bright side,' said the P.D. 'Within a few minutes you had had your first rabies injection. If you had been bitten in Colombo or, say, in some distant village, the delay would have been much longer and perhaps with awful consequences.'

After a day or two Sarah became more reconciled, although she found the morning injections a little embarrassing, because the doctor had to inject her stomach. Dr Coomasaru was discretion itself and thoroughly professional, however, and injected Sarah quickly and efficiently. As soon as she straightened out her dress the doctor would draw up a chair and would have a ten minute chat with his patient. Sarah appreciated these little talks, because they were of a reassuring nature and were largely confined to getting Sarah fit and ready for her wedding.

Sarah soon found herself happily planning the wedding and the hundred and one accompanying details with Andrew. The only thing that really began to worry her was the amount of shopping she had to do for her trousseau. As usual, Angela Sanders came to the rescue by forestalling her worries.

After Sarah had had her fourth injection, Angela said, 'Sarah, dear, you're not going to have a lot of time to buy your trousseau, are you?'

'It's something that's been worrying me quite a lot, but I'll have to manage somehow.'

'I've had an idea. I had it yesterday, in fact, and I've made some tentative arrangements which you may or may not like. Peter thinks it's a good idea!'

'Why do you spoil me like this? Please tell me your idea.'

'Well, one of my best friends in Colombo is the wife of our Agents' senior partner. Her name is Jane Scott, and we've known each other for years. I phoned her yesterday and told her all about you and your wedding. To cut a long story short, Jane says why don't you spend a couple of days with them in Colombo before Andrew comes down? She will take you shopping and you will be able to get a lot done before you have to meet your parents, because you won't have much time after that. As I say, Peter likes the idea, and he will arrange for Dr Coomasaru to give you your final three or four injections to take with you for the Colombo doctor to administer. Andrew will come down in the Buick as already arranged. What do you think?'

'I think you're an angel. You know, only last evening, when I was saying goodbye to Andy after dinner, we both talked about how simply marvellous Mr Sanders and you have been. Andy said that ever since he came to Strathmore you've treated him as if you were his parents.'

'We're very fond of you both, but there's just one little snag,' said Angela. 'Would you mind going down to Colombo, to the Scott's house, in the estate lorry? It's not very comfortable, but the driver is first class and he'll deliver you safely to Jane's home.'

'No, of course I don't mind. I can't thank you enough for arranging all this. It's such a load off my mind.'

The lorry drive to the Scott's house was uneventful although Angela's warning about discomfort was true. Jane Scott was waiting for Sarah and gave her a warm welcome. The house was a lovely old Dutch bungalow, very large and spacious, with a huge garden leading off the back verandah. Flowers were everywhere, but what caught Sarah's attention were the enormous lawns, bright green, and the many large trees, some with scarlet blossoms. Sarah just stared, and then she turned to her hostess. 'What are these little green birds?' she asked.

'Parakeets. They fly in every evening and by early morning they've gone again. It's a lovely garden, isn't it? Derek and I love it here. Now come inside and I'll show you your room. You must be longing for a shower or a bath. But perhaps you would like to telephone your fiancé first to tell him you've arrived safely.'

'Thank you, I would,' said Sarah. 'You know, it's a funny thing, but I've hardly given him a thought since I left Strathmore. I was so busy enjoying the trip down to Colombo and thinking about the hundred and one things I must do before he comes down to meet our parents on their ship, that I've hardly given Andrew a thought!'

'I'm not surprised,' said Jane Scott. 'You must have so much on your mind. Now, this is your room, and your bathroom is through that door. Don't hurry. I don't expect my husband back for another hour or so.'

Sarah unpacked and got ready for her shower. She was surprised that she had thought so little of Andrew all day. She forgave herself quickly, remembering that, as Jane had said, she had had so much on her mind since leaving the estate.

She had a cold shower, changed, and found Mrs Scott sitting in the garden with her Boxer dog at her feet.

'This is Thuni, after Thun in Switzerland, where Derek and I honeymooned.'

'I wonder if I may telephone Andrew, Mrs Scott? I feel a little guilty at neglecting the poor boy!'

'Of course, my dear, come with me!'

Sarah was soon chatting away and she felt penitent when Andrew told her that he missed her terribly, and that she had been in his thoughts all day. She felt all her old passionate love coming back while she spoke, and she told Andrew how she longed for the time to pass so that they would be together again.

The sun was thinking of setting and Sarah and her hostess were sitting on a verandah chatting, when Derek Scott arrived home from the office. Jane Scott made the introductions and the head boy arrived to take orders for a pre-dinner drink.

'I'm going to call you Sarah, if I may,' said her host. 'And now I've one or two things to tell you. I've been in touch with Mackinnon Mackenzie, the agents for your father's ship and, of course, they're all ready for the arrival of their Chairman. They are sending one of their larger launches to meet the ship and they suggest that they take you and your fiancé out with them. Knowing you would agree, I've cancelled our launch. Mackinnons have also put a large car and driver at your parents' disposal for as long as they are in the island. I know you have made the necessary reservations at the Galle Face Hotel, and I know that our Strathmore superintendent, Peter Sanders, has put his car at Andrew's parents' disposal. Finally, the ship's agents have arranged for one or two parties to welcome the Allenbys but you'll be hearing all about the social activities in due course. I'm just going to have a quick shower and get out of these office clothes, and I'll be back.'

After a drink or two they moved into dinner and Jane said that Sarah would be called at half past seven in the morning, for breakfast at eight o'clock. Then they could start their shopping soon after nine, as there was so much to do.

Sarah was awake well before her early morning tea was brought in, because the crows outside her window were in full cry. Though it was not only the crows that had woken her. She had been sleeping lightly since the early hours with some disturbing thoughts. She felt that she was beginning to panic about her wedding. She felt suddenly alone and longed to be with her mother again.

She told herself not to be silly, and that her feelings were more likely to be the reactions that Dr Coomasaru told her she might expect from the rabies injections.

Sarah had breakfast with Jane Scott, who outlined her plans for the day.

'First, Sarah, we must go to my husband's doctor who will give you your rabies injection at half past nine. Then we will go shopping – you tell me what you want, and I'll take you to the proper shop.'

Sarah liked the new doctor in Colombo who gave her the injection. She mentioned the feelings of depression and uncertainty that she was feeling since she came down to Colombo. She told the doctor that the estate doctor had warned her of a possible reaction to the injections, and he replied that he was surprised, and he didn't think Sarah's depression had anything to do with the injections.

The day went quickly enough, and Sarah was surprised at the amount of shopping she was able to do. The two ladies lunched lightly at the G.O.H., a hotel near the port, and resumed their tour of the shops till late afternoon.

When they returned home, they sank exhausted into comfortable chairs on the lawn while they had tea and watched the parakeets arriving.

After tea, Sarah rang Andrew and explained that she was not feeling too well. She told him not to worry about it, and that she felt sure that the cure she needed was to see him in about forty-eight hours time.

The forty eight hours were the longest Sarah could remember. She tried to bring back her enthusiasm for the wedding and for all the excitement that awaited her. She tried hard not to show her despondency and worry to the Scotts, but she knew they must suspect that something was wrong. Jane Scott was kindness itself and did all she could to help her guest.

'Sarah,' she said, 'I know exactly what's wrong with you, because I went through exactly the same trauma when I was getting ready to marry Derek. And I had my mother to help me! You haven't even got that comfort, although very soon now you will have your parents here to go to. They will assure you that all is well, and that your worries are perfectly normal.'

Jane Scott's words had little effect, and Sarah found she dreaded going to bed that night because she knew she wouldn't sleep. Her worst moment came in the early hours when the awful realisation came to her that, first, she no longer loved Andrew and, secondly, she could not possibly go through with the wedding. She cried herself to sleep an hour or two before her early morning tea was brought to her.

It was now the Scotts turn to be worried. Sarah looked as if she was on the verge of a nervous breakdown. She looked very ill, she wouldn't eat and they hoped that Andrew's arrival that afternoon would help.

Andrew was to spend that night with his old friend Martin Phillips, with whom he had spent his first night in Ceylon. Before driving to Martin's house, Andrew told Muttusamy to take him to the Scotts' bungalow. Sarah was lolling in a long cane chair on the front verandah waiting for him. He dashed out of the car and they embraced.

After only a few moments, Andrew pushed Sarah gently away. 'Sarah, my darling, what on earth is the matter? You look ill, very ill. What is it, darling. What has happened?'

Sarah put her hand to her head. 'I don't know, Andy' she lied. 'I'm feeling dreadful. I can't sleep, and I don't want to eat. I'm so sorry to greet you like this.' She pulled out her hankie and covered her eyes.

He led Sarah on to the verandah. Jane Scott tactfully kept out of the way, although she had seen the young couple meet.

When Sarah had seated herself, out of sight of Muttusamy, Andrew knelt at her feet. 'My darling, darling Sarah, tell me what's wrong. What's happened? When did you start feeling like this?'

'I can't explain, Andy. At first I thought it was my rabies injections, but the doctor down here is sure that it isn't. I explained to him on my first visit that I wasn't feeling well, and he said it was nothing to do with the injections and that he was quite sure it was a case of *crise des nerfs*, the result of all the things on my mind, the awful lot of shopping I had to do and so on. I feel better already, having you by my side again, and I'm sure that when I see my Mum and Dad tomorrow morning, I'll be quite OK again.'

'I hate to leave you like this, darling. I feel so helpless. I wish there was something I could do. I'll say goodbye now, and I'll see you by the launch on the passenger jetty tomorrow morning. Get well soon, my darling, I can't bear to see you like this.'

Muttusamy had seen a little of the meeting between Andrew and Sarah, and he knew something was wrong. His fears were confirmed when he saw Andrew approaching the car. Andrew sat in front, his head bowed.

'Something is wrong, *Dorai*, I know it. I hope nothing serious. I will say a little prayer.'

Andrew touched his shoulder. 'Thank you, Muttusamy.'

Martin Phillips had not come home from the office when Andrew arrived at his bungalow. However, the head boy was expecting him and showed him to his room. Andrew concentrated only on Sarah in his shower and also while he dressed for the evening. The shock of seeing her as she was an hour or so earlier had numbed him, and he was desperately worried. He had hardly recognised the distraught young thing that greeted him. In just a few days she seemed to have changed into a nervous wreck.

After Andrew had left, Sarah went straight to her room and broke down. She had recovered herself to some extent by the time dinner was served, but her host and hostess were deeply shocked to see the state she was in.

Sarah's host was the first to speak. 'My first reaction, when I came home and saw you, was to immediately send for our doctor. But then I remembered he had said, when he injected you, that this was a form of nervous crisis and that it would pass. I think the tonic you need is to be hugged by your parents tomorrow. Then you will know that they are with you and that you can go to them at any time right up to your wedding morning with your worries. Jane agrees with me.'

'I'm sure you're right,' said Sarah, 'and I can only apologise for being so boring while I'm a guest in your house. I'm so sorry. I don't know what's hit me, but I must confess that I am longing to see my parents again.'

The next morning, when Sarah was dropped at the passenger jetty by the Scotts' driver, she saw Andrew at once. He came hurrying forward and opened the door for her. They embraced and Andrew was relieved to see that Sarah looked a little better than the afternoon before.

'Andy, I'm feeling much better this morning, and I'm so very sorry I was in such a state yesterday. If only I could sleep properly I'm sure it would help a lot. I'm so sorry,' she repeated. 'This must be a great disappointment for you.'

'Never mind that, darling. All I want is to see you as your old, wonderful, happy self again. I'm so thankful you're going to see your parents any minute now. It's going to make all the difference, I know.'

They moved inside and down a flight of stairs to where the ship's Agents' launch was waiting. Martin Phillips greeted Sarah enthusiastically and the coxswain held her arm as she climbed aboard. Martin introduced Sarah and Andrew to the others already on board, and the coxswain headed for the great white liner anchored in the middle of the harbour. It was still fairly early morning on a lovely sunny day and it was still pleasantly cool.

Sarah and Andrew spotted their respective parents at once. They were standing near the gangway watching the launch approach. As the crew moored the launch to the pontoon alongside the ship, Andrew helped Sarah off the launch and let her lead him up the gangway.

The Allenbys and the Harveys greeted their young with great joy and affection, and the two families moved towards the swimming pool area. After a few minutes it was agreed that the Allenbys and Sarah would go down to their stateroom, and that the Harveys would take Andrew to theirs. They arranged to meet again at the gangway in an hour's time to go ashore.

As Andrew's father closed their cabin door, his mother turned a very worried face to her son. 'Andy, is Sarah all right? She looks ill – very ill. When we met her briefly in London before she came out to you, she was such a pretty, sparkling young thing. Full of life, so much in love with you. I hardly recognised her just now. Has something gone wrong?'

'I don't know, Mum, I really don't know. When she left me on the estate a few days ago she was exactly how you have just described her. Full of life and sparkling. When I saw her yesterday afternoon in Colombo I was horrified. She was tearful, she looked so ill and I'm sure she's on the verge of a nervous breakdown. She told me just now that she was feeling a little better this morning, and she's longing to be alone with her parents to pour out her troubles. If only I knew what these troubles were. I hardly slept last night. I'm so worried.'

'Was she ill on the tea estate?' asked Andrew's father. 'Did she seem unhappy or worried there?'

'No. As I've just said, she was full of life and so excited. But there is something you don't know. Last week Sarah was bitten by a mad dog on the estate. Mercifully we were just a few hundred yards away from the estate hospital, and the doctor was there. Within minutes he had given Sarah the first of her ten or twelve anti-rabies injections and he assured her that she would not develop rabies. However, he warned Sarah that she might get some mild reaction from the injections. However, our Agents' Colombo doctor, who has given Sarah one or two of her remaining injections, has said that her trouble has nothing to do with rabies. He says she's very tense and anxious about all the arrangements for our wedding. He called it a *crise des nerfs*, I think.'

Sarah's parents were even more worried. They had never seen their daughter look so ill, and slowly and patiently they extracted as many details as they could from her about her dramatic change.

'You still love Andrew, I hope?' asked her mother.

'This is the awful part, Mum, I don't think I do. I don't want to marry him. I don't want to go ahead with the wedding. I *can't* go ahead with it. I'm so worried and unhappy I can't sleep. I know how badly I'm going to hurt Andrew when I tell him. He's going to be devastated. What has happened to me? It was all so sudden: one minute I loved Andrew with all my heart. I couldn't wait to marry him, to live with him forever; and the next minute, my love for him vanished. I must tell him now that we must cancel the wedding and that I'm going back to England with you.'

'Sarah, darling, just hold your horses for a little while,' said Sir Colin. 'Rest assured that no one is going to make you marry if you don't want to. But I feel quite sure that this is just a temporary hiccup. I cannot believe that your deep, deep love for Andrew can evaporate overnight. Whilst you've been talking I've had an idea. Sitting at our table for dinner were two wonderful people: Sir Richard and Lady Barlow. He is a well known neuro-specialist and Lady Barlow is equally well known as a psychoanalyst. In their circles they are world-famous, and your mother and I have got to know them very well during the voyage. So have Andrew's parents, who also sat at our table. This is a heaven-sent opportunity. Please let me talk to them about you. I don't think they've left the ship yet. Let me do this, Sarah, please.'

'Dad, please do anything you like. I'm desperate. You do the thinking. I can't think of anything at present except this awful illness I have.'

Sir Colin picked up the phone by his side, and his call was answered by the neuro-specialist himself.

He listened to Sir Colin explain the situation with only a few interjections, and then he said, 'Hold on a minute while I talk to my wife.' After only a moment or two: 'I've spoken to my wife and she and I will be only too happy to see you and your daughter at once. Where can we meet?'

'This is very kind of you, Richard, but when are you going ashore?'

'Not until after lunch, so we have a lot of time to see your daughter.'

'Well, bless you. May we expect you here in ten minutes or so?'

Sir Colin then rang the Harveys and told them what was happening. He said that he hoped the Barlows would have finished with Sarah before lunch, and he suggested they all lunched together afterwards to exchange notes.

The Harveys were very relieved that such a couple as the Barlows were going to examine Sarah, and said they would wait anxiously for Sir Colin's next call before lunch.

The Barlows arrived at the Allenby's stateroom and were introduced to Sarah. Sir Colin asked whether they would like to be alone with Sarah, but they declined, saying it would be good for Sarah to know that her parents were by her side.

Sarah explained exactly what had happened since she arrived on Strathmore: how ecstatically happy she had been; how deeply in love she had been with Andrew; how impatient she had been to marry him. Then, soon after she was bitten by the dog, her feelings changed dramatically, and now she no longer loved Andrew and the very thought of marriage horrified her. All she wanted was to stay with her parents and go back to England.

The Barlows listened in silence and then Sir Richard asked, 'Have you any of the rabies injections left? Oh, and have you had a blood test?'

Sarah said she had an injection in her bag, and that she was intending to ask the ship's doctor to inject her. She said she had not had a blood test.

'I'll take that injection off you, I think, Sarah,' said Sir Richard. 'I would like to have the contents analysed. I don't expect anything will be wrong, but it may be old stock or something, and by having it analysed we will have ruled out one possibility.' He turned to Sir Colin. 'I wonder if you would ring the ship's doctor? I'd like you to tell him briefly what's happening, and say that I have asked for blood samples to be taken from your daughter. He can send the nurse up here to do it.'

Sir Colin moved to the phone and in a few moments the doctor himself knocked on the door. He took samples of Sarah's blood and said he would be able to report on his findings within the hour. Sir Richard asked him if he could arrange for a rabies injection to be analysed.

'No, I'm sorry, I can't do that,' said the doctor. 'I haven't the facilities. I think the ship's Agents – they're on board now – could have the analysis done by the Government Analysts here. Give me the injection, if you will, and I'll see what I can arrange.'

After the doctor had left, Sir Richard and his wife talked to Sarah for well over an hour. When they had finished they excused themselves and said they would be back in quite a short time. They were as good as their word.

'My wife and I find ourselves of the same mind,' said Sir Richard.

'We both realise that Sarah is seriously disturbed mentally. It's her mind that is causing the trouble. You can forget the dog incident, and we are virtually certain that they will find nothing wrong with the injection. We are equally positive that Sarah's blood test will be perfectly satisfactory. We think loneliness is perhaps the one major factor that has caused the trouble. There has been so much on her mind, and she has not had either of you to go to discuss things with. Then, Sarah has been in a strange country, in a strange environment, in a strange climate. Unknown to her, she has had to bottle up all these different conditions. She has had no safety valve, so to speak, by which she could let off steam. A minor contributory cause could be that she has been living at a very high altitude – nearly six thousand feet – which can affect the nervous system. Then suddenly, in a matter of four or five hours she finds herself at sea level in Colombo. It could well be that this sudden change released all the pressures that had been building up inside her and that is why she had such a dramatic change of heart as soon as she arrived at Mr and Mrs Scott's house. Well, that is our diagnosis. Now here is our suggested remedy. You will think it is a paradox – perhaps it is – but we recommend you try it. Shall I tell you what my wife and I recommend?'

'Of course, please do, at once! We shall do whatever you say,' said Lady Allenby.

'Well, here goes,' said Sir Richard. 'My wife and I have made it plain that we think Sarah has had this breakdown – for that is what it really is – as a result of the circumstances in which she had been living at a very high altitude. Now, here's the paradox. We want you to take her back there – if not to the tea estate itself, then to a place called Nuwara Eliya. By a strange coincidence, we are spending a fortnight at the Hill Club in Nuwara Eliya, and you will love it. But, if you can arrange it we would like Sarah to go back to Mr and Mrs Sanders on the tea estate and Andrew to go back to his duties. We feel that this will "exorcise the devil", and that Sarah, knowing that her parents are at hand, will unconsciously look at things quite differently. You see, the things that have been a strain on her will seem quite different with you both close by. We ask you, seriously, to do this. Although my wife did most of the talking on deck just now – not unusual, I can say – we found we were both of exactly the same mind. And, of course, we have had some experience of these things.'

'Coincidences seem to be the order of the day,' said Sir Colin. 'My Company's Agents in Colombo, in collaboration with Andrew's superintendent on the estate, have already booked my family and the

Harveys into the Hill Club until just before the wedding. Sarah has told us that Nuwara Eliya is less than an hour's drive from the estate. However, we are not going up country for two or three days. There's so much we have to do in Colombo before we leave for the hills.'

'Absolutely ideal,' said Lady Barlow. 'Particularly the fact that we shall always be on call. We would love to see Sarah from time to time, to see how she's getting on.'

Lady Allenby put her hand on her friend's arm, 'How can we ever thank Richard and you for all you are doing for us? It's providence at work. Whatever the outcome, we shall always be in your debt.'

'Say no more,' said Sir Richard, 'but there is one thing. Will you please bring the analyst's report on the injection when you come up to Nuwara Eliya?'

The Allenbys said that yes, of course, they would be pleased to do so.

The party moved down to the main lounge, where an anxious Harvey family was waiting for them. Sir Colin did all – or most – of the talking, and by the time he had finished, the Harveys were fully in the picture. Andrew had chosen a seat beside Sarah, and although she seemed glad of this, there was none of the spontaneous joy and excitement that would have been the case a week earlier.

'I must telephone my P.D.,' said Andrew. 'He knows nothing of all this. I'll ring as soon as we go ashore.'

'Telephone from here, Andy,' said Sir Colin. 'The ship can afford it!' He turned and winked at the neurosurgeon. 'It's quite useful being Chairman!'

Andrew excused himself and went to the radio office to see if they could connect him to Strathmore. They could, and he was soon talking to Peter Sanders.

He told his P.D. about Sarah's terrible mental breakdown, and he confessed he had never been so saddened and distraught in all his life.

Peter's reaction was immediate. 'Would you like a few more days Colombo leave?' he asked.

'No, sir,' said Andrew. 'We are all coming up-country the day my leave expires. Sarah's family and mine are booked in at the Hill Club, and I shall be in my bungalow that evening. But there is something I'd like to explain, and then I'm going to ask Mrs Sanders for a very special favour.'

'She's by my side now, Andrew. Just hang on a moment and she'll go to another phone and then you can speak to us both.' There was a short pause. 'Carry on, Andy, I'm listening,' said Angela Sanders. 'Start from the beginning, because I missed the first bit.'

Andrew did as he was asked and then said, 'I'm heart-broken, Mrs Sanders. I was terribly shocked when I saw Sarah on my arrival at the Scotts' house yesterday afternoon. I hardly recognised her, and I felt she hardly recognised me. She was tearful and very distant. I almost felt that we were meeting for the first time. She was a little better when we came on board this morning – in fact I'm speaking from the ship now. We've had a wonderful piece of luck, which has helped us all. A couple of specialists, a man and his wife, are travelling on this ship, and they have been sitting at the Captain's table with my parents and Sarah's parents so they all know each other. When the Allenbys saw Sarah a little while ago they were as shocked as I was, and then Sir Colin had a brilliant idea. He telephoned the specialists, a Sir Richard and Lady Barlow, and explained what had happened to Sarah. They came down to the Allenby's stateroom in a matter of moments and sort of took charge. They first had a long talk with Sarah, and then told us that she was suffering from a serious mental breakdown. They put this down to the probability that Sarah felt lonely on Strathmore without her parents. They felt she had so much on her mind with the wedding and the other hundred and one things that she had to do, and she didn't have her parents on hand to unload and discuss problems with them. Finally, she broke down and they seem convinced that this is the result. The Barlows have now recommended a possible cure. Surprisingly, they think Sarah should come back to Strathmore and to carry on exactly the same as before she came down to Colombo. This time, though, she'll have her parents at the Hill Club. Mrs Sanders, can I possibly ask you to have Sarah to stay for another week or ten days? I feel very selfish in asking you to be so kind, but I'm desperate, and the Barlows seem quite sure that their idea will work.'

'Andrew, say not another word,' interrupted Mrs Sanders. 'You bring your Sarah here as soon as you can. And another thing – Please tell your parents and the Allenbys that they are to treat Strathmore as their own home, and they are to come here as often as they like. I only wish we had enough room to put them all up. After all, though, the Hill Club is only an hour away. Be brave, Andy, and count on us to do all we can. I'm going off to have a good cry!'

'I've been thinking whilst you've been talking, Andrew,' said the P.D. 'I'll get hold of Doctor Coomasaru and put him in the picture. I'm sure the poor man will be worried stiff that his patient has had a breakdown. He'll be wondering if anything he did was wrong.'

'Please tell him, sir, that the Barlows are convinced that neither the dog bite nor Coomasaru's injections have anything whatever to do with Sarah's troubles. Just as a precaution they are having the injections analysed to see if they are old stock, and they have given Sarah a blood test. I'll tell him the results when I see him.'

Chapter 10

A few days later the Allenbys and the Harveys left Colombo for Nuwara Eliya in cars provided by Sir Colin's people. Sarah and Andrew drove up to Strathmore in the Buick, driven by the faithful Muttusamy. The drive to the estate was quiet, and was quite different to the last occasion when Andrew had just taken Sarah off her ship and was driving her up to Strathmore for the first time. In fact, this time it was Muttusamy who added some fun and entertainment on the long journey up-country. He seemed to be fully aware of the sadness affecting his two young passengers, and he kept up a steady flow of comments and anecdotes which helped more than he could have imagined.

Stock and Trigger were in equally good form, and squealed with delight when they saw Sarah. She would have been knocked flat had Andrew not steadied her.

Angela Sanders brought the two dogs to order and embraced Sarah. 'Come in, my dear, and rest. Andy, we'll expect you for dinner.'

As Andrew left with Muttusamy, Sarah said, 'Can we just sit and chat for a little while before I change? There's so much I want to tell you, so much I want to apologise for.'

'There's simply nothing to apologise for, darling Sarah. All Peter and I want is to see you back again to your old, sparkling, happy form. As we told you one evening after dinner, we look on Andy and you as part of our family. Peter is lurking around here somewhere. He didn't want you to have too big a reception committee when you arrived. Let's find him, and then you chat away as much as you like.'

They found the P.D. and settled down for tea. Neither host found it easy not to show signs of their alarm at Sarah's appearance. It shocked them to see the deterioration that had taken place in a little over a week.

'I must say, first of all, that when the specialists on the ship strongly recommended – almost insisted – that I should come back to

126

Strathmore, my reaction was to rebel. I couldn't bear the thought of putting you to all the inconvenience and trouble of nursing a nervous wreck. You both have been so kind and generous to me. I'll never forget that evening, after dinner, when Andrew proposed to me and you gave me your engagement ring to wear. I must now return it because Andrew has given me my permanent one.' She held up her hand. Then she bowed her head and the Sanders saw from her shoulders that she was sobbing.

Angela Sanders rushed to her, put an arm round her and sat on the arm of her chair. 'Darling, what is it? Whatever is the matter?'

Sarah raised a tear-stained face. 'I hope it's this wretched breakdown that's doing this to me, but I don't love Andrew any more. I can't go through with the wedding. I've told my parents this and I was going to tell Andrew, but my father persuaded me to wait. He seemed sure that my sudden change of heart was the direct result of my nervous breakdown. He was confident that as I recovered, so would the deep, deep love – indeed, the adoration – I had felt for Andrew would return. So Andrew knows nothing except he must see that things have changed dramatically. So I'm wearing his ring and I hope – I so hope – I never have to take it off and give it back to him.'

'Sarah, your father is quite right,' said Peter Sanders. 'I *know* he's right and I, too, am quite sure that in a very short while you will be your wonderful, happy self again. I say this because I'm certain that the fact of having your parents here will do the trick.'

As for Andrew, his feelings can be imagined. He was heartbroken: there was no need for Sarah to tell him that she no longer loved him. It was all too obvious, and he knew their engagement was over. He knew it was only a matter of time before she told him herself, and gave him back the engagement ring. He was just considering whether it would make things easier for Sarah if he made the first move that night, and make it easier for her to break off the engagement.

He was wondering what course of action to take when his telephone rang. It was the estate doctor, and he was very agitated. He explained that the P.D. had spoken to him a few days earlier and told him how very ill Sarah had been. Dr Coomasaru said that the rabies injections had been mentioned more than once and, although Mr Sanders had said that he need not worry because no blame had been attached to him, he *was* worried, very worried, and for his own peace of mind he would like to see Sarah as soon as possible.

Andrew understood how the doctor felt, and he said he would see what he could do, although, he warned him, he didn't think Sarah was in any mood to see anyone.

Dinner was a pretty sombre affair and there was no talk of the engagement being broken off. Andrew mentioned that Dr Coomasaru was very worried and that he would like to see Sarah. To his surprise Peter Sanders reacted favourably at once.

'I'm glad this has happened, Andrew, and I'll tell you why. Please listen, Sarah and try and agree with what I'm going to say. Now, we all know what you are going through and we can fully appreciate your feelings. But, for the last day or two, and with no prompting from Coomasaru, I thought it would be a very sound idea if he saw you for a short time every morning. He could watch your progress and he would then be able to report to the Barlows at the Hill Club on a daily basis. The Barlows could then advise Coomasaru on what he should do. Please agree, Sarah, because all we want to do is help you, and this seems a good way for you to have regular attention.'

'I'll do anything you say, of course. I know everyone is trying to help me, and I'm very, very grateful. When would the doctor like to come?'

Mrs Sanders said, 'I think he should come every morning after breakfast, and spend some time with you.' This was agreed and Coomasaru and the Barlows were more than happy when they were told of the arrangement. The Barlows were particularly pleased because they knew they would now have a fully qualified medical report every day on Sarah's progress.

Dr Coomasaru arrived punctually at nine o'clock the next morning. As usual, he was immaculately dressed in a white drill suit, and he was met on the front verandah steps by Peter Sanders.

'Before I take you to Sarah, I can give you some news that will put an end to your worries. Firstly, the analysis of the injection showed nothing whatever wrong and, secondly, Sarah's blood test was absolutely clear. So Coomasaru, you have done nothing wrong and Sarah has had a nervous breakdown brought on by her forthcoming marriage and the many, many things she had to worry about without her parents to help her. The load was too much. Come inside.'

They found Sarah sitting comfortably in a cane chair on a side verandah and greeted the doctor. He came forward and shook her hand.

'Well, I'll leave you both,' said the P.D. 'Ring for anything you want.'

The doctor drew up a chair near his patient. 'Miss Allenby, I think

I'm on the verge of a nervous breakdown myself. Since I heard about your illness a few days ago I've been distracted with worry. But already I feel a little better, because Mr Sanders has just told me that there was nothing wrong with the injections I gave you, and that the result of your blood test is first class. I'm also so thankful that your specialist friends are at the Hill Club, and I can report on your progress every day. Now, may I take your pulse, please, and your blood pressure?' After a few moments he said, 'Your pulse is normal but your blood pressure is a little high. Nothing to be alarmed about, and I am not going to prescribe anything. I'll simply report to Mr and Mrs Barlow every evening and do whatever they advise.' He put away his things and turned to Sarah. 'Miss Allenby, tell me a little about yourself, your early school days, your family, what sports you enjoy, what pets you keep. I just want you to lean back comfortably and chat to me.'

The doctor drew her out and, to Sarah's surprise, she found that half an hour had passed before he rose to leave. 'I'll see you again at nine o'clock tomorrow, Miss Allenby. Just relax and see as much as you can of Mr Harvey. He's a fine chap, a very lucky chap, and he will make you a fine husband very soon.'

Soon after the doctor left, Angela Sanders came and sat down opposite Sarah. She held out a switch key. 'Andrew looked in very early this morning, before you were awake, and gave me this. It's the key of his M.G. and he says it is at your disposal. He does not need the car for a few days, and he wants you to keep it and treat it as your own, so that you can drive up to the Hill Club whenever you want to be with your parents. He really is a very thoughtful young man. Are you still "out of love" with him?'

'I'm feeling better this morning, better than I've felt for some time, but my love for Andrew is dead. I know he's a wonderful person – I was besotted with him and I adored him – and then suddenly it all went. To me, now, he's just a nice young man. I hate the thought that I'm hurting him so badly. There's nothing wrong with my memory. I remember how we first met on the ship; I remember how quickly I fell in love with him; I remember how lost and desolate I felt when he left the ship to work here and I sailed away with my parents. I remember how ecstatically happy I was when I knew I was coming out to stay with you here. And then Andrew proposed to me here, under this roof, and I nearly died of joy. You do understand, don't you, that I'm not making all this up? I simply can't pretend to Andy that I still love him. I don't. I can't marry him. Oh, what am I to do?' She buried her head in her hands and burst into tears.

* * *

Andrew threw himself body and soul into his work. He felt some relief in tiring himself out, and he found that a state of near exhaustion somehow dulled the ache in his heart. Underneath his despair he knew, with certainty, that Sarah's present attitude towards him was the direct result of her illness. He prayed and hoped that he was right and that, as she got better, her love for him would return. The thought of going through life without Sarah was unbearable, and if her love for him did not return, he knew he would have to do something drastic. He realised he could not go on alone.

When Dr Coomasaru arrived for his second morning's visit, he didn't need Sarah to tell him that she was feeling better. He could see it in her face and in her eyes. The stress was not so evident.

Sarah shook him by the hand. 'I'm feeling so much better,' she said. 'I had a full night's sleep last night for the first time in ages and, for once, I'm beginning to feel that life is not so bad after all! Do I look better?'

'You certainly do, Miss Allenby, and while I'm glad for you, I'm even more glad for myself!'

'What do you mean?'

'I mean that you started your breakdown after I gave you those wretched rabies injections. I know now that there was nothing wrong with them, but I can't shake off this feeling that these injections started your troubles. Professor and Mrs Barlow speak to me very kindly on the telephone and, last night, when I told them of my feelings of guilt, they told me not to be silly! Anyway, now let me take your blood pressure and listen to your heart so that I'm ready for my evening report to the Barlows. Are they a "Sir" and "Lady" Barlow?'

'Yes, they are,' said Sarah.

Although the doctor had a surgery at 10 o'clock that morning in the estate dispensary, he found that Sarah had so much to say for herself that he had to excuse himself and hurry back to his patients. He was greatly relieved at Sarah's progress.

After the doctor had left, Sarah found Mrs Sanders. 'I'm feeling so much better that I think I'll take Andrew's M.G. and have lunch with my parents in Nuwara Eliya.'

'A very good idea. You're looking a different person this morning, and I think it will do your parents a world of good if they can see your improvement for themselves. Off you go and I'll expect you back when I see you. Why don't you leave a little note for Andrew as you go past his bungalow? He's feeling very, very low, you know, and I think a note from you will cheer him up.'

Sarah found it hard to write the note. She wanted to sound endearing, her old affectionate self. Instead, on her first effort she sounded formal and distant – but she had better luck on her second attempt.

Sarah thoroughly enjoyed her drive to Nuwara Eliya, and her mother was delighted to see her improvement in health. After they had embraced she said, 'We knew you were coming, darling, because we telephoned Strathmore about half an hour ago and Mrs Sanders told us you were on your way. She also said you were feeling better, and now I can see that for myself. Much better! I'm so thankful. Dad has gone with the Harveys to look at a tea factory, but they'll be back for lunch. Let's sit on the front lawn in the sun. I want to hear your news.'

They settled themselves comfortably, and a Hill Club steward brought them coffee. 'How are your feelings about Andrew, darling?

'Just the same Mum, which is so very disappointing. I had so hoped that as I started to feel better that my love for Andrew would come back. It hasn't. It's not that I dislike him or anything, it's just that I see him as a nice young man and nothing more. I know for certain that I can't possibly marry him. One of the reasons why I came up here to see you this morning was to ask you to cancel the wedding. I simply can't go through with it, Mum. I'm so desperately sorry, I really am.' She looked for her handkerchief.

'We knew it was going to come to this, darling. The only thing that we are not sure about is when we should cancel all our arrangements. Mercifully, the list of wedding guests is not very big – it's quite small, in fact. The thing that worries Dad and me most is the Harvey family. Poor Andrew, we were so happy for you. We think you could not have found a better husband. We can see no fault in him. The Harveys are being very brave, but I know what they must be going through. We were all so excited on the ship, discussing our plans, and now, suddenly, it's all over, finished, done. We sail home with our tails between our legs. It all seems such a tragedy, but there it is. Your feelings must come first, and not only that, it wouldn't be fair on Andrew if you married him while you were only pretending to love him. We'll talk it over when the others come back, and then we'll make a plan. Darling, it breaks my heart to see you so unhappy.'

Before lunch, the Allenbys, the Harveys and the Barlows discussed the problem for an hour without coming to any definite conclusion. They agreed to let matters drift for three or four more days, until the end of the week in fact, and then they would take whatever action was necessary.

Sarah went back to Strathmore and stopped at Andrew's bungalow on her way to the Sanders. Andrew was not at home, but Muttiah, Andrew's boy, made her comfortable and said that he was expecting his *Dorai* at any minute.

Andrew's heart leapt when he saw his M.G. in the drive, and he could see Sarah on the verandah. He rushed to her and they embraced for a moment.

Then Sarah pushed Andrew away gently. 'Andrew, I can't forgive myself for what I'm doing to you. To say "I'm sorry" means nothing. I know how much I'm hurting you and I'm hating myself for it. There's nothing, simply nothing, I can do about it – and I have tried. I've tried very hard.'

'Darling Sarah, I'm heartbroken, of course. I can't believe that our wonderful love for each other has suddenly disappeared, and I can only pray and hope that something will happen to bring it back again. At least I'm encouraged by seeing you looking so different. You look so much better, so much happier. Perhaps your love for me will start returning soon. Do you think there's any hope?'

'Andrew, I wish there was. If I could only feel a small spark re-kindling itself I'd be overjoyed. I wish I could understand what has happened to me. Even the Barlows don't seem to know what's wrong. I'm feeling much, much better, but there's no love.'

Sarah sat down and motioned Andrew to sit beside her. 'I had lunch with your parents, my parents and the Barlows at the Hill Club today.' She broke off. 'Oh, Andrew, I haven't thanked you for lending me the M.G. It's so sweet of you, thank you very much but I'm afraid I won't need it much longer.'

'What do you mean?' Andrew asked slowly. 'Tell me, please, although I know what you're going to say.' He covered his eyes with his hands.

'Yes, Andy, my parents have decided to go back to England at the end of the week. I am to go with them. We are not going to cancel anything until then but, if my feelings haven't changed by then, I'll come and tell you first. I'll come and say goodbye!'

'You mean, our engagement will be broken?'

Sarah couldn't speak. She could see the hurt and the sadness in Andrew's eyes. She just nodded. She gave him a quick peck on the cheek and fled. Andrew watched her start the M.G. and drive off. He sat and thought about himself. He knew that his life as a tea planter was finished – although he thought he might have to complete his five year agreement – but after that he would leave Ceylon for ever.

The Sanders did what they could to amuse Sarah for the rest of the evening but without much success. She felt so wretched and sad, nothing in the world seemed to be able to get through to her.

When Sarah awoke the next morning she was surprised to realise that she had had a remarkably good night. More surprisingly, for a reason she couldn't fathom, she felt somehow elated. All she knew was that she was looking forward to the usual morning visit from the estate doctor.

Dr Coomasaru arrived punctually at nine o'clock, looking his usual immaculate self. Sarah went forward to meet him and took his hand. The doctor seemed embarrassed and looked away shyly. 'Miss Allenby, you mustn't do that. I'm only the estate doctor, you know, and Mr and Mrs Sanders would be shocked if they had seen you hold my hand.'

Sarah led him towards the corner of the verandah they usually occupied. 'You may be the estate doctor, but I bet that no other estate has such an immaculate, debonair and handsome medical officer.'

'Miss Allenby, please, you mustn't say such things. If Mr Sanders had heard you say that he would give me the sack.' He looked round nervously to see if they were being watched.

'Come and sit down,' said Sarah. 'If only you knew how good these visits are for me. I look forward to them a great deal, and I only wish they were longer.'

'Miss Allenby, I don't know what to say except that I am simply a servant of the estate, and you must treat me as such. If you can't do that, you must treat me as your doctor and only that. I'm trying very hard to make you feel better because I still have this uncomfortable feeling that your illness started when I gave you your injections. I'd feel much worse if I didn't have Sir Richard and Lady Barlow to speak to every evening to report on your progress. They keep on assuring me that I am not responsible in any way for your illness.'

'Of course you're not. Far from being responsible for my illness, your visits are doing me a lot of good. As I've just said, I look forward to them.'

'How did you sleep last night?' asked Coomasaru, opening his medical bag and looking intently at Sarah. 'I don't think I needed to have asked that question. Your eyes are clear, your colour is good and you look happy – yes, you look happy.' He did his usual tests and put his instruments away, finally turning to look at Sarah. 'What shall we talk about this morning, Miss Allenby?'

'You,' said Sarah. 'I want to talk about you. I feel so calm and happy when I'm near you. I can feel myself relaxing. Why should this be, "Doctor"?' She used the word with a coy emphasis.

'Miss Allenby, you say I make you feel happy and relaxed. Well, you make me very nervous and uncomfortable. Suppose the servants are listening?'

'Hang the servants. They aren't listening anyway. I think you have this wonderful effect on me because I feel you are out of place as an estate doctor. I see you more as a fashionable specialist in London with consulting rooms in Harley Street. I rather like that image. Then I could come and see you on some trumped up illness and you could examine me thoroughly. From head to foot. I'd like that too!'

'Miss Allenby . . .'

'Oh! stop calling me Miss Allenby. My name is Sarah!'

'Miss Allenby, please, you must stop this or I will have to go. You are engaged to Mr Harvey, and what would he think had he heard what you've just said?'

'I no longer care what he would think. I'm no longer in love with Andrew and, for your information only, I don't think I'm going to be engaged to him for very much longer!'

'Have you quarrelled, Miss Allenby? What can possibly have happened to make you break off your engagement? I hope you are only joking.'

'No, I'm not joking, far from it. but since I've had this illness – or breakdown, or whatever you like to call it – I've lost my love for Mr Harvey. I'm so sad because I know just how much I've hurt him. More than that, I think I've broken him. I don't think he'll stay in Ceylon after we've gone.'

'You mean you are going to leave us?'

'Yes, my parents and Mr Harvey's parents have decided to sail back home again at the end of the week if, by that time, my old passionate love for Andrew hasn't returned; and I can't believe it will.'

Coomasaru was silent for a few moments. He rested his hand on Sarah's. 'I'm so sorry to hear this, Miss Allenby. I shall lose my favourite patient.'

'I'm glad you said that, Mervyn. Yes, don't look so shocked, I'm going to call you Mervyn. Yes, I'm happy too that you called me your favourite patient, because you are very much my favourite doctor!'

Coomasaru snatched his hand away. 'This is getting out of hand, Miss Allenby. You're making me very nervous and embarrassed. I shall have to stop coming to see you if you go on like this.'

'Oh, don't be silly, Mervyn, I'm not really serious. It's just that I've been through such a bad time that I enjoy your visits a lot. Do you mind if I flirt a little with you?'

'It scares me, Miss Allenby. I really must be going.'

He packed up his bag and almost ran down the steps to his car.

Angela Sanders found Sarah strolling in the garden. 'Sarah, darling, I'm going to drive over to Halgranoya, the other side of Nuwara Eliya, to lunch with a girlfriend of mine. She would be delighted if you would come too.'

'Thank you very much, but really, I'm such poor company just now that I'd be a wet blanket and spoil your lunch. Please forgive me, but I'd really rather stay here.'

'I quite understand, Sarah dear. I'll be back for tea.'

Sarah went on walking in the garden, stopping now and then to admire the spectacular views. The sun was flooding the tops of the hills to the west, and the thousands of tea bushes provided a vast emerald green tapestry. While she strolled, Sarah was examining her thoughts. These seemed to be concentrated exclusively on Dr Coomasaru and she realised, with a shock, that she was becoming very fond of the Strathmore doctor. She moved to a garden bench and gave her thoughts full rein. Could this possibly be true? she wondered. Why should I start falling in love with another man so soon after I had dismissed Andrew Harvey from my affections? Mervyn Coomasaru was striking in appearance. He was very dark, tall and with the physique of an athlete. His 'tiger' eyes set off a very handsome face. His features were perfect. But, most of all, thought Sarah, it was his tender, shy and comforting manner that appealed to her. I shall lose my favourite patient, she remembered him saying. The recollection pleased her.

The Sanders were pleasantly surprised at the dramatic change in Sarah at dinner that evening. She was very nearly back to her previous form when she first met the Sanders. They remarked on this, but Sarah just smiled and made no mention of the Strathmore doctor.

After another very good night's sleep, Sarah was sitting on the verandah impatiently waiting for Mervyn Coomasaru to arrive. He was punctual as usual.

'Good morning, Miss Allenby,' he said, and they settled themselves in their chairs as on all previous mornings.

'Miss Allenby, this morning we must only talk about your condition. I feel very uncomfortable at some of the things you said yesterday. You were treating me as if I was your boyfriend. I am not, you know.

I am only the Strathmore estate doctor and you must please treat me as such.'

'I love it when you become stern and get on your high horse and lecture me on how to behave, and how to treat you. You make me love you all the more when you do this. There, now I've said it and I'll say it again. I think I love you, Mervyn.'

The doctor sprang to his feet. 'Miss Allenby, please stop. You don't realise what you're saying. It's not possible for you to love me. I am only a servant of this tea estate. If anyone else hears you talk like this I will be sacked on the spot. Think what your parents would say, and what they would do, if they heard you say that you loved me.'

'They would be shocked and very worried, but they would soon realise that it was all part of my illness. In any case they would know that we all leave for England in a few days' time and that my infatuation would soon pass. What they would not know is that, perhaps, this is no infatuation. As I've just said, Mervyn, you mean a great deal to me and this fact has made me feel much better. I don't know what I shall do when we leave for England. Perhaps you will find that you love me, too, and you might ask me to stay.'

'If only it was possible that I could ask you to stay, but you must see that our positions are so different. Now, I must examine you for my evening report to the Barlows.'

Sarah telephoned her mother as soon as the doctor had gone. She invited herself to tea and said she hoped the Harveys and the Barlows would also be there because she had something very important to say.

'Say it now, darling. What is this important something? I hope it's good news. Please say it is. Please say you've begun to love Andrew again.'

'Not quite that, Mum, but what I am going to tell you has made me very happy, and I hope it does the same for you at tea this afternoon.'

It was a very happy lunch that the Allenbys, the Harveys and the Barlows enjoyed that day. Everyone gave their own opinion as to what the 'important something' was that Sarah was going to tell them at tea. The general opinion was that Sarah, though not quite fully in love with Andrew yet, had begun to feel the first flickering of the flame. They felt sure that Sarah would ask for a postponement of the plan to cancel the wedding and to sail for England at the weekend.

Sir Richard Barlow went a step further: 'I'm so glad we recommended that Sarah should go back to the tea estate and be close to Andrew. We felt quite sure that, being near him, would bring back her love.'

'If you're right, Richard, our debt to you will be incalculable,' said Colin Allenby.

They were all impatient for Sarah's arrival. At last they saw the M.G. approaching the Hill Club. Sarah left the car by the front porch and ran on to the verandah where the party had assembled. Before she even spoke it was plain to see that she was radiant again. The sadness and stress had left her: she was back to her old, vital self again.

Sarah embraced her parents first and then greeted the others.

'Wonderful, darling, simply wonderful,' cried Sarah's mother, hugging her again. 'Now, we all want to hear your good news. You're in love again, aren't you?'

'Yes, I'm in love again, ecstatically in love again. I'm so happy!'

'I imagine Andrew is equally ecstatic, isn't he?' said Sir Colin.

'No, Andrew is not happy. He's not happy because I'm not in love with Andrew. I'm head over heels in love with someone else.'

The stunned silence on the verandah seemed to go on forever and it was Sarah's father who broke the spell.

'I'm not sure I understand what you've just said, darling. You said that you're in love with someone else. There *is* no one else. Who can there be?'

'I'm in love with the Strathmore doctor, Mervyn Coomasaru. He is the gentlest, kindest man I have ever known. He is the man who has cured me, brought me out of the nightmare I've endured for the past weeks. I've felt better, stronger, happier, after each of his morning visits, and I adore him. I want to stay here and marry him.'

There was another silence. Anthea Harvey clutched her husband's arm and put her handkerchief to her mouth. After a moment she spoke. 'You mean you have no love left for Andrew?'

'I would give anything for all this never to have happened, Mrs Harvey. I know what I've done to Andy. I know full well just how terribly badly I've hurt him. I know just how shocked you must all be that I've changed so abruptly: that, in a matter of days, I could possibly switch off one great love and transfer it, in all its intensity, to another man. I've thought about this, morning, noon and night and I simply can't help myself. I love Mervyn, and I want to marry him.'

The Hill Club servants arrived with tea and were sent away.

Sir Colin said, 'Darling, you say that you've thought about all this, morning, noon and night. Have you considered such things as where you will live, and how you will live on a tea estate doctor's pay? What nationality your children will be, and how they will feel as they grow up not being quite one nationality or the other? There are countless more things that we must consider. Your parents still love you, you know, and as your parents we must have the right to talk this whole affair over with you. I think you must move into the Hill Club with us tomorrow so that we can talk things over calmly and try and agree what is best for you. Does this doctor love you?'

'I'm not sure. He's so shy and modest and self-effacing that I'm not sure. He's never said that he loves me. He gets embarrassed whenever I mention love to him. When I told him this morning that I was in love with him, he cut short our visit and fled. It's his kindness, his modesty and humbleness that I love. He's so conscious of his position as compared to mine. He kept on saying that he is only a servant of the estate. He keeps on saying that our positions are so vastly different. He is terrified that he would be sacked if the Superintendent got to hear that I loved him.'

'That's all very well – I've nothing against this man – but your mother and I are only concerned about you. I think your love, as you call it, is no more than an infatuation, and something that will pass as quickly as it came. I am convinced I'm right, because after a few weeks or months living on a tea estate as Dr Coomasaru's wife your infatuation will die. Anyway, darling, we all need time to think and by tomorrow morning we will see if we can come to your point of view. So, please explain to Mr and Mrs Sanders what has happened; tell them everything about your love for the estate doctor – how we feel about it, how concerned we are – and that we want you to move into the Hill Club with us in the morning. Please do that.'

Sir Colin went on, 'And another thing. Does Andrew know about all this? Does it occur to you that he has the right to know that his fiancée has fallen in love with the estate doctor? You must tell him today before you come up here tomorrow. Will you promise me, please, that you will do all these things.'

Sarah couldn't speak. She just nodded, kissed her parents and ran to the M.G. Despite her promise, she knew she wouldn't be able to tell the Sanders anything before she told Andrew.

When the sound of the car had died away, Richard Barlow was the first to speak. 'I feel so terribly guilty about all this. Had we not suggested – recommended – that Sarah should come back to the estate, this would never have happened. I take full responsibility and I will do anything you suggest to try and put things right. I can only apologise from the bottom of my heart to both families for the terrible mess I've made of things. If I hadn't stuck my oar in, this would never have happened.'

'You're not quite right there,' said William Harvey. 'I think you've forgotten that Sarah was already ill before you met her on the ship. We were all shocked, if you remember, at Sarah's appearance, and it was clear to us all that she was very, very ill. Please don't look on this latest development as your responsibility.'

As she had done once before, Sarah stopped at Andrew's bungalow on her way to the Sanders'. Andrew was at home and he rushed to the M.G. before it had even stopped. To his horror he saw that Sarah had been crying and was very unhappy. He took her arm and led her to the verandah.

'Andy, I promised you when we sat here the other day that I would tell you myself if I found I still didn't love you.'

Andrew sat quite still.

'I don't love you, Andy, and I don't know what's happened to kill the total devotion I had for you until a little while ago. I am not just saying this lightly, because I know how much I'm hurting you, and I hate myself for it. I'm in love with someone else. It's only just happened, a few days ago, but I know I'm in love with this man.'

'Who is it?'

'It's Mervyn Coomasaru, your estate doctor.'

Andrew just stared at her.

'Tell me this isn't true, Sarah. How can you possibly be in love with him? You've only known him for a few weeks. Have you been having an affair with him? Have you been going to see him? I can't believe it. Say it's not true.'

'It is true that I love him Andy, and he has had nothing to do with it. I mean he has not made any of the running. I have fallen in love with Doctor Coomasaru's gentleness, his humbleness, his kindness and the tremendous amount of good he has done me. Oh! I can't explain it all, Andy, and I'm so sorry. My parents are shocked and stunned. I am to leave Strathmore in the morning to stay with them at the Hill Club. Don't ask me any more questions Andy; all I know is that I'm in love. I'll never forget all the happiness we've had together. Please drive me back to the Sanders' and then keep the M.G.'

139

Chapter 11

Andrew didn't sleep at all that night, and could hardly concentrate at all on his work the next morning. He arrived at his bungalow for lunch as usual, and he saw a single letter on the verandah table. It was addressed to him and the envelope was of a deep cream, almost yellow colour and the ink was green. The handwriting was strange to him and, tossing his hat on to a chair, he sat down to read the astonishing contents.

Dear Mr Harvey,

You do not know me and I have never met you, but I must write this letter.

Your estate doctor is Mervyn Coomasaru, and he is my ex-husband. He is a murderer and a bigamist, and a very evil man. I know these things, although I was only married to him for a few months. During this short time he was perhaps faithful to me for the first week or so. Then, until I divorced him, he had a string of women with whom he would confront me, and then boast of his sexual capacity. He seemed to enjoy shaming me like this. His appetite for women is insatiable.

Perhaps, this time, my ex-husband has gone too far. I will explain. Last week I was shopping and one of Mervyn's ex-women came up to me. She asked me if I had heard of his latest conquest. She said that he had been sexually attracted to an English girl on a tea estate and that she was falling in love with him. He was quite sure she would soon want to marry him. I found out that the estate was Strathmore and I also found out that this young lady is engaged to you.

Beware, Mr Harvey, Mervyn is a very dangerous man. He is also a very good actor. He can be very shy and humble. He only does this to get what he wants. Don't believe him, don't let your young lady go anywhere near him. I will give you some good advice. Confront him with this letter. He will recognise the paper and the writing. Do this in public, in front of his boss and your fiancée. Do it now, before it is too late.

I wish you well.

Andrew sat still. He was in a state of shock. He only roused himself when his boy reminded him for the second time that his lunch was getting cold. He was in no doubt that the letter was genuine. He now knew that Sarah was in love with Coomasaru. He knew it would only be a day or two before she broke off their engagement and cancelled the wedding. Strathmore seemed to have a curse on him. There had been one drama after another ever since he arrived.

After eating hardly any lunch, he moved to a long cane chair on his verandah wondering what to do. He decided to keep the letter away from Sarah and his parents for the moment and, instead, to see his P.D. as soon as he could. He telephoned the big bungalow and Angela Sanders answered. After a short chat she called Peter to the line.

'You sound worried, Andrew. Come up here at once and tell us all about it. Have you got your M.G. or has Sarah got it?'

'Sarah returned it yesterday evening, sir, and thank you once again. I'm always worrying Mrs Sanders and you, and there seems to be a jinx on me. I'll come at once.'

The Sanders were waiting by the front steps when Andrew drove up. Angela embraced him. 'You poor, poor boy. What is it now? You can't stand much more of this. What has happened? Come and sit down.'

Andrew handed his P.D. the letter. 'Please read it out aloud, sir. I'd like Mrs Sanders to hear it as well. I only got it an hour or so ago when I went back to my bungalow for lunch.'

The Superintendent read slowly, and aloud, and no one spoke for a minute or so after he had finished.

Peter Sanders broke the silence. 'Andrew, don't be surprised but I have a strange feeling that this letter might be good news. What I mean is, that Sarah must read it at some stage. I think it might break her infatuation with this bloody man, or, if it doesn't break it, it will surely dent it quite seriously.'

'I think Peter is right,' said Angela Sanders, after a pause. 'I'll try and arrange a dinner party here for this evening. I'll ask your parents, Andrew, and the Barlows and Sarah's parents. And, of course, Dr Coomasaru. I think when he sees who is coming to dinner it will be Coomasaru who will have the nervous breakdown! And yet I find it hard to believe what's in that letter. Dr Coomasaru is such a gentle man. Sarah says she is in love with him, I know, but he has always been so gentle with her, so caring, so concerned about her breakdown. I simply can't believe that letter. I'll see if I can arrange this party for this evening.'

Great good fortune attended Mrs Sanders' efforts. She had to drive into Nuwara Eliya that afternoon in case she had to do some shopping for the party, and as she was very near to the Hill Club she drove in. All the people she wanted were having tea, and so she was able to arrange her dinner party with no trouble at all. Coomasaru accepted her invitation at once over the telephone. His hostess gave him no indication as to whom his fellow guests would be.

That evening the party forgathered in the drawing room of the Superintendent's bungalow and, much to the Sanders' surprise, the doctor seemed perfectly at ease. He seemed to have eyes only for Sarah. Having greeted her parents and the others, Sarah moved over to the doctor. There was no doubt at all that their relationship was almost intimate. The Allenbys were devastated, the Harveys were horrified and the Barlows were mortified that their plan to send Sarah back to Strathmore had so clearly failed. The situation was now much more dangerous than it had been. The only redeeming feature was that Sarah seemed totally recovered in her health.

She and the doctor didn't seem to talk much, they seemed just to stare into each other's eyes in infatuation.

The sense of embarrassment in the room was almost overpowering. Neither host nor hostess, nor their guests, could take their eyes off Sarah and the doctor for long. Angela Sanders soon decided she had to break the tension and she signalled her head boy to serve dinner.

The party seemed fairly relaxed during the meal, and the hostess had taken care to seat Sarah as far away as possible from Dr Coomasaru. As coffee was being served, Andrew took the yellow envelope out of his pocket and laid it beside his coffee cup.

Almost at once Coomasaru got to his feet and bowed towards his hostess. He left the room and was back in a few moments. 'I'm so sorry about that, Mrs Sanders. You see, I'm a diabetic and suddenly I had to give myself some insulin. I'm fine now. Please forgive me.' He looked across at a worried Sarah. 'I'm quite all right now, Sarah, I really am.' He sat down appearing to look a little embarrassed.

Andrew picked up the yellow envelope and withdrew the letter.

At once Coomasaru pushed back his chair and stood up. All eyes were turned on him. 'Yes, yes, I see what you're holding, Harvey.

Look, I have one myself. I got it in this morning's tappal bag. A tappal bag is a post bag,' he explained to the puzzled guests from England.

Peter Sanders put down his coffee cup quite sharply. 'What do you think you're doing, Coomasaru? Please sit down at once. You're disrupting our party.'

'I'll sit down quite soon, Mr Sanders, but not just yet. There's something I'd like to say. Mrs Sanders, will you please dismiss the servants.'

Looking very puzzled, Angela Sanders nodded to her head boy and the servants left the room.

Sarah was staring at the doctor with a shocked expression. He seemed suddenly to have lost his gentle demeanour. His 'tiger' yellow eyes were suddenly cold in his very dark face, and he seemed to know that he had the undivided attention of the whole table. They just stared.

'The letter that Andrew Harvey is holding matches the one in my hand. They should match because they have been written by the same person, and I'm quite sure the contents of both letters are very much the same. In fact I know they are the same, because my wife has told me what she has written to Harvey.'

Andrew got to his feet.

'Sit down, Harvey!' ordered Coomasaru in a voice that Sarah didn't recognise and which Andrew at once obeyed.

The doctor went on: 'These two letters have altered many things, many important, vital things. If you will all please listen with patience and without interruption, I'll explain. The letters are from an ex-wife of mine and she has heard that Miss Allenby is in love with me, so she has decided to expose me. Hence the letters, and in them she accuses me of being a murderer and a bigamist. A bigamist, yes I'll admit to that, but as for being a murderer, well, the silly girl died more from fright than from what I was doing to her. I'm still a doctor, however, and I think Miss Allenby is about to faint. Someone give her some brandy.' He went on: 'I left my last job as a doctor on a rubber estate in the low country because the police were uncomfortably close to me. I thought that by coming to Strathmore I'd shake them off. I'd reckoned without my ex-wife, because she has told the police where they can find me. Now, I must explain that my sexual appetite is uncontrollable. I chose tea and rubber estates to work on because there are hundreds of women employed on them. I could pick and choose whoever I wanted whenever I wanted. There was never any shortage. Miss Allenby attracted me the first time I met her. Then, when she was bitten by that dog, and I started giving her the rabies injections, I knew that I would have to make her mine. She would have to be at my beck and call and that, whenever I wanted her, she would have to be there to . . . to, er . . . oblige me. I realised the odds were against me, but I knew I could succeed.'

He looked at Sarah. 'Your colour is coming back. Have another sip of brandy. I'm nearly through.'

Coomasaru looked down the table at his spellbound guests. 'Now, where was I? Oh, yes, the seduction of Miss Allenby.'

A chair was pushed back violently. 'Sit down, Sir Colin,' barked the doctor. 'For your own good, let me finish. Well, I've told you that I wanted to have Miss Allenby at my disposal whenever I needed her. I was not in love with her. I never have been in love with her.'

Sarah put her napkin to her eyes and covered them.

'It was pure lust,' he went on, 'nothing more. Just lust. I only wanted her body.'

Coomasaru looked towards the Barlows. 'I've been told, Sir Richard, that you and Lady Barlow are world-famous in your particular fields. Well, you haven't impressed me at all. You've diagnosed Miss Allenby's ailments as stress, nervous breakdown, neurosis, home-sickness and goodness only knows what else. What rubbish! You never thought of hypnosis. You should have done. You're not very observant. I have that power and I needed it to succeed. You see, I had to do two things to Miss Allenby. First, I had to make her "fall out of love" with young Andrew Harvey here and then, when she had done that, I had to make her fall in love with me. You must admit I've succeeded pretty well, although, at one stage, I had to bring a second power into play. This second power was a form of spell. I learnt about it from an old Fakir in Central India during a sabbatical some years ago. I won't explain – you'll only scoff – but you can see the result for yourselves.' He stopped and finished his coffee. Nobody moved. 'Now, you can all relax. Andrew Harvey has, by the power of that letter in his hand, made me change my plans and intentions quite dramatically. Please listen carefully. Miss Allenby is now completely free of all the influences I've put her under. Please believe me, in forty-eight hours or less she will be radiant again, radiant because her passionate love and devotion to Andrew Harvey will have returned in full force. By tomorrow morning she will start feeling for Andrew again. Before dinner this evening I had Sarah to myself for fifteen minutes. I had her quite alone and, in that short time, I broke all the influences and control I've had over her. I must say I couldn't believe my good fortune when she came back to Strathmore after her Colombo visit. She came back on the advice of the Barlows. I had her to myself for almost an hour every morning. During that time I first started to make her turn from a disregard for Andrew to a passionate love for me. I made her love me; she was under my spell. But now you have my assurances – you simply must believe me – Sarah will be back with her Andrew, and madly in love with him, in a day's time or less, and the wedding can go ahead as planned. You must all try and forget everything that has happened since that day. I made it happen and now it's over. I hope, I really do, that Sarah and Andrew will be very happy.' He turned to Angela Sanders. He waved his ex-wife's letter. 'This has destroyed me. I have to confess to a small lie, Mrs Sanders. I am not a diabetic, I did not take insulin just now. In fact I injected myself with a massive, lethal, dose of morphine' – he looked at his watch – 'and I have about forty minutes to live.'